War and Suits
Two of Clubs

J.A.Armitage

Heather

Don't let the dragons like you away

Armitage

Contents

January 1st

The sound of snoring drilled through my brain in much the same way as a bulldozer would pass through cement leaving me no choice but to open my eyes to nudge whoever, or whatever, it was making the godawful racket into quietness. I sighed as I took in the state of the scene before me. It was worse than I had expected. Thousands of wine-stained glasses, plates full of half-eaten canapes, knives, forks, and spoons reminded me that there had been the biggest party of the year here last night. The banging headache reminded me that I'd drunk too much at it. Empty wine bottles littered the floor amongst the remnants of party poppers and streamers and what inexplicably looked like a pair of discarded panties, pink with pretty, little ribbons on them. No prizes for guessing whom they belonged to! The smell of fireworks lingered in the air, mixing quite horribly with the stench of leftovers.

I followed the sound of the noise to a pile of coats in the corner. The coats had been left on coat hooks by the guests at last night's party, but many had fallen to the floor giving an opportunistic partygoer a bed for the night. I pulled back a couple of layers of coats to find my older brother Tarragon, curled up with a Heart girl. I didn't know her name, but I'd seen her around She had to be one of the royals, but which one? It couldn't be a higher royal. Maybe she was the Two like me, but I could have sworn I saw some younger Hearts last night. Trust Tarragon to sneak a Heart into the kitchen. The New Year's celebrations were held yearly in an attempt to bring the four clans together. Whilst this was my first party as an official member of the royal family, I'd seen enough of the aftermaths of them to know that a lot of handshaking and promises of change happen on the night itself, but by the time February rolled round, we were all at each other's throats again. Ever since the dawn of time, or at least the beginnings of Vanatus, the four ruling clans had maintained a very tenuous grasp on peace. At least we'd managed to hold off on all-out war since way before I was born.

I nudged Tarragon with my toe.

"GGrrnngggrrr"

I sighed again. The New Year was already off to a bad start as far as I could see, and my head felt like it was being put through a cheese grater. Reminder to self, just because you get the opportunity to try alcohol for the first time, doesn't mean you have to try all of it at once!

I looked down at Tarragon and his lady friend.

The Hearts, Diamonds, and Spades were supposed to be kept to the nicer parts of the castle. No one was supposed to see the kitchens. Not that I suspected the sleeping Heart girl currently wrapped around my elder brother actually cared what the state of the kitchen was. Still, our father, the King, would be upset that someone from one of the other clans had seen that we weren't the perfect royal family we proclaimed to be and that we did, in fact, have messy kitchens - very messy this morning. Who would get the blame for this? Not Tarragon, that's for sure. Tarragon was only the Four of Clubs, but he was one of Father's favourites. I, on the other hand, was the lowliest of all. As the Two of Clubs, I ranked only slightly higher than the mice that sometimes frequented the kitchen despite the hard work of Fluff, the palace cat. And it was I who would get the blame for this.

I glanced at the Heart woman. Usually, you could tell a Heart from the clothes they wore, the most ridiculous 'high fashion' which usually consisted of a lot of lace, tulle, feathers and leather, but as I couldn't see the rest of her, I guessed that she was completely naked under the heap of coats. She was unmistakably a Heart, though. Even with a lack of clothes, I could tell. Red hair fell in waves down the flawless porcelain skin on her naked back. She looked perfect and sensuous in every way, another rather annoying trait of The Hearts. They just didn't have bad hair days!

"Oy," I whispered to my wayward brother. The drill-like snoring turned into a grunt so I stuck a toe in his side.

"Wha...? Oh, it's you!" He actually closed his eyes again, pretending to fall right back asleep. He was in for a shock if he thought I was going to leave him here.

"Will you get her out of here, please? I have to clean the kitchen to get it ready for the cooks." I might have been the lowest member of the family, but I'd developed into someone my mother described as ' a wilful child' and my father called 'a pain in the ass'. Tarragon knew he had no chance of being left alone with his new plaything.

"What time is it?" He opened his eyes again. His chin was damp with dribble, and he had streamers still weaved through his hair like a multicoloured wig. I couldn't resist giving him an eye roll.

"It doesn't matter what time it is. If father catches you with her, there will be hell to pay, and I don't want to be involved. Why did you bring her down here anyway? She could be a spy." Unlikely, as she'd actually been invited to the castle along with the rest of her family. And unless The Hearts had a secret desire to learn how much kitchen cleaner we used (not a lot it seemed), then the chances of her being sent down here to spy were slim. Still, Tarragon didn't need to know that.

"Why do you think I brought her down here? Can you not see her? She's gorgeous."

I scowled. His complete disregard for the rules irritated me. It didn't matter how beautiful the woman was, she was still a Heart and therefore completely untrustworthy. If her father caught them together, well, it didn't bear thinking about.

"She's a Heart!" I stated the obvious, knowing that Tarragon was fully aware that she was a Heart, and that was more than likely the reason he'd bedded her in the first place.

"Isn't this whole party thing to get the clans together so we can cooperate and live in a peaceful land? This is why we all come together at this time of year." He gave that leisurely grin that women of all races seemed to fall for. It wasn't going to work on me, though. I was mad!

"Yes, but I don't think that you are supposed to come together quite so literally!"

"Or quite so many times," grinned Tarragon.

"I feel nauseous enough already, thank you!" I pulled a face before rummaging around in the pile of coats.

"Hey," Tarragon sat up alarmed. "What are you doing?"

"I'm looking for her dress. I assume she did actually have clothes when she came down here?"

The woman awoke and gave a seductive smile.

"Good morning," she purred. Oh god, she was good. Just the sound of her voice made me quiver, thanks to The Hearts ability to seduce anyone they meet. A swift flick of my eyes to my brother told me that she was having the same effect on him. Hopefully, I didn't have the same stupid, dribbly expression on my face as he was currently exhibiting.

I turned away on the pretence of searching for the dress but, in actuality, was completely embarrassed by the nudity of this strange woman who had sat up and was now barely covered.

Seriously, did this woman have no modesty? These Heart women were certainly something else.

"I'm Journey," she paused whilst she stretched leisurely and yawned, "Number Eight if you are interested."

"Rose," I answered, not looking back at her. I didn't particularly want her knowing my name, but if she was a royal, which she'd just confirmed she was, we'd be formally introduced at the meeting later, so I might as well try and be civil now.

I wasn't interested, as such, about her place in her family. I was more concerned about getting the woman dressed and out of the kitchen, but I was surprised. Heart woman very rarely batted below their own rank. Even just one number down was unusual. The Hearts coveted power above all things and sleeping with someone below your rank was not the best way of getting it. I knew that this was a one-night thing, and Tarragon would be under no illusion that this particular liaison would turn into something long-term. He probably didn't care. He'd be boasting about bedding this woman for weeks. The thought made me want to vomit even more than the excess of mead I'd consumed, and I made a mental note to avoid him until he found something else to talk about. He was going back to university in a couple of weeks. I wondered idly if I could manage to avoid him completely until then. With some luck and good management, it was possible.

"Did you happen to have a dress with you?" I asked as politely as I could muster. Journey laughed. It was a sensuous laugh, husky.

"I think it's over there." A manicured talon with a heart neatly painted on it pointed across the room.

I swiftly turned to look where she was pointing. Journey had stood up, and obviously the word modesty wasn't in her vocabulary at all. She was completely naked except for a gold necklace and the highest red heels that I had ever seen. Golden tattoos sparkled on her body, even in the low light of the kitchen. Swathes of golden flowers, inked from the curve of her right breast swirled down her side before curving inwardly and coming to a stop just below her belly. Her left arm was also decorated in a similar fashion. The woman almost glowed.

'Show-off' I thought maliciously. My own tattoos, the ones of The Clubs, were black, discrete, and extremely boring in comparison.

The dress, a backless black silk gown had been flung across the room and was hanging from a light fitting at the other side. It was surprisingly unfussy for a Heart creation although none of the other suits would wear something as revealing and overtly sexual as this in public. I hurried to get it and passed it to Journey who, thankfully, shimmied into it quickly.

"Thank you." Journey smiled. Her lipstick was still perfect from the night before, a slash of crimson on alabaster skin. Not a strand of hair was out of place. She picked up a black bag covered in what looked like peacock feathers and diamonds, blew a kiss at Tarragon, and left through the back door without another word.

"Wasn't she special?" The lovesick puppy look was still on his face. What a moron!

"Get up! I need you out of here, and for God's sake, put on some clothes."

"I seem to have misplaced them," he said apologetically before picking up a frying pan to cover his modesty and bounded up the stairs to the main palace.

I sighed for the third time that morning. That was one mess cleaned up, now to the important task of cleaning the other. Usually, the palace cooks would be in charge of the kitchen, and they would have bevies of servants to clean for them. But as last night had been New Year's Eve, my father had let them leave early, as soon as the evening banquet had been prepared. Having never once stepped foot in the palace kitchens, and grossly underestimating the mess that over fifty people enjoying themselves could make, my father had decided not to pay the triple wages (which was the going rate for New Year's Eve) and decided his youngest daughter could do it. I had to clean it quickly before the palace cooks arrived at ten to prepare a feast for the top royals before midday.

The royal families of all of the clans were due to eat in precisely three and a half hours, and at the moment, I couldn't even see the stove for dirty plates.

"How am I going to be able to pull this off?" I asked Fluff, who had appeared at my side, begging for food. I rarely wished to be anything other than a Club, but I would have quite happily traded places with a Diamond this morning, if only for their magical capabilities. Had I been a Diamond, I could have magicked this all up. Unfortunately, I wasn't, and the little Club magic I possessed wouldn't have cleaned a spoon, let alone a whole kitchen. I found a plate with most of the contents left on it and put it on the floor for the cat to eat.

Catching my reflection in the mirror, I groaned. I was nothing compared to the beautiful woman that had just vacated the kitchen. I didn't have time for makeup, and I knew that if I tried it, I'd have panda eyes from mascara and any lipstick would have ended up halfway up my cheek. Even without the disaster of makeup, I was still a mess. My hair, which my sister, Star, had spent hours brushing and braiding into a perfect chignon, was now a mess of knots, and I had a piece of lettuce stuck to my cheek making me look like I had a particularly nasty skin condition. At some point the night before, someone had spilled red wine down my pretty, green dress. Worst of all, I must have fallen asleep on yesterday's copy of The Club Gazette and had the headline, along with the picture of the Queen of Hearts printed across my face.

I sighed once more and, not for the first time, knew I wasn't cut out to be a princess. My race, The Clubs, were not known for being the prettiest beings in Vanatus, but even compared to my own kind, I still managed to look scruffy most of the time. My next oldest sister, Star, had tried her best with me; but as Tarragon had told me only half-jokingly the night before, you can't polish a turd. I'd have been upset with him, but I secretly agreed. My sisters, though lacking the beauty of The Diamonds, the overt sexuality of The Hearts, or the ability of the shifting Spades to change appearance at will, at least had the charm and breeding of ladies fit for the Royal Court. I, however, never quite managed the grace and poise of my elder sisters nor the good looks. Although, I had to admit, Star had done a pretty good job of making me look almost feminine the night before.

Last night was the first time I'd worn a dress since I'd learned the word 'no' in retaliation to my mother trying to force me into yet another hand-me-down dress that my sisters had grown out of. We might have been royalty, but our land was small, and eleven children cost a lot to clothe. As the poorest of the four suits or races, we, as royals had to lead by example, which meant I often wore something that had been worn by at least three of my sisters before me. At a young age, I decided I'd prefer the leftover clothes of my brothers, much to my mother's despair, and since then, I'd been more than content to wear green pants and a simple tunic. It wasn't the attire of the princess I was, but the clothes of the warrior I wanted to become. That day was a long way off, though, and I was much too young to attend the knight's school where my eldest brothers spent their days, learning how to wield a sword and skewer an enemy with a lance. Until then, I'd resigned myself to the fact that I was the one who had to clean when the servants had a public holiday, and that meant starting on the kitchen.

I would have cried if it wasn't for the appearance of my oldest brother, Sage, and older sister, Sorrel.

"Hey, sis," called Sage. "We came to help. Oh god, what a mess!"

I'd never been so happy to see my elder siblings.

"Why is The Queen of Hearts jumping off a lettuce leaf on your face?" asked Sorrel, pulling off the offending article and discarding it on a nearby plate.

"I fell asleep on The Gazette."

"Thank goodness, for a second I thought you'd got a new tattoo!" Sage laughed, and I ran to him to give him a hug. I was infinitely glad I'd already managed to clear out Tarragon and Journey. Sage would tell our parents for sure, or he would reprimand Tarragon himself.

"What are you doing here?" I asked. Sage was the Jack of Clubs, which meant that he was the heir to the throne. Kitchen tasks were way below his rank.

"We thought that you could use a hand," answered Sorrel, the Nine of Clubs. "Sage will have to leave to put his peacock suit on soon enough, but I can stay and help." She pulled a piece of green ribbon from the pockets of her simple shift dress, and tied her long dark hair into a ponytail.

"You don't need to. The servants will be here soon enough, and I can get this done pretty quickly."

Sorrel surveyed the mess and raised an eyebrow in an exaggerated fashion.

"Ok," I conceded, laughing. "Perhaps I could do with a little help."

Between the three of us, we had the whole kitchen clean and ready for the kitchen staff within an hour. The bins at the back of the palace were overflowing with bottles, but the kitchen itself gleamed like new.

Sage bade us farewell and went to change into his royal attire, or what we younger royals like to call his peacock suit, as it was aquamarine in colour.

"Do you think I'm pretty?" I asked my sister when we finally managed to find five minutes to make ourselves a cup of coffee. Prettiness was not something I had ever thought about before. But remembering the lithe limbs and tight body of Journey, not to mention the perfectly sensual face, had made me question my own looks, and now I felt woefully inadequate.

Sorrel smiled kindly at me. Worrying about being beautiful was not something she'd ever have to do with her perfectly straight hair, flawless skin, and a natural hint of pink about her cheeks.

"Of course, you are. What makes you ask? You're not usually one for questions of vanity."

I weighed up whether to tell Sorrel about The Heart woman that Tarragon had brought into the kitchen. I could never have told Sage about it, but Sorrel would probably understand.

"Tarragon had a woman down here. I caught them here this morning. She was a Heart."

"Ah," exclaimed Sorrel as if this answered my question. "Let me tell you something about the Hearts. They are all stunningly beautiful. It's all they care about, power and beauty or at least the appearance of it. They dress in the most seductive of apparel, they drape themselves in gold, and they adorn themselves in jewels that they buy, steal, or coerce out of The Diamonds. You'll never see a Heart without makeup on. It isn't a coincidence that their city has the highest concentration of clothing shops and makeup parlours. But you have something they could never hope to possess. You have the beauty of innocence. Even with your hair all over the place, as it is now, no one could hold a candle to you. I would bet my royal title that this Heart woman would be jealous of your youth and your fresh-faced beauty."

I sorely doubted that the woman I'd seen earlier would have anything to be jealous of, let alone lowly Rose Club who barely made the grade as a royal. I was a least a foot shorter, had pointy ears, had lettuce mixed with print on my face, and was wearing a red-blotched dress as an inadvertent fashion choice. Still, I loved my big sister for trying to cheer me up.

"It's easy to fall in love with a Heart, too easy," continued Sorrel, "But it's not easy to keep them. The irony is that their family name is Heart when all they do is break them."

Sorrel looked off into space as if she was thinking about someone. I didn't want to let on, but I knew it was the Eight of Hearts. She'd had a very brief, secret affair with him a couple of years ago and had not dated anyone since. For the briefest of seconds, I saw pain in her beautiful face, and I wondered if I'd ever find love that would affect me so much.

"Your highnesses, I think you'd better come upstairs. We have a problem, and The Queen requests your presence."

I looked up the stairs to see, Tree, the head courtier. He had the manners of a gentleman and the face of a pug, and as sometimes happens within some Club Families, he had a tinge of green about him. He saluted stiffly and turned to leave.

Problems with Mother? Uh oh. She'd spent weeks trying to make our castle look better than it actually was in an effort to keep up with the other royal families. It was an utterly pointless endeavour as the castle was draughty, green from both moss and ivy, and in places, falling down. I'd never seen the royal courts of the Hearts, Spades, or Diamonds, but I was willing to bet that theirs didn't have wobbly staircases and staff that were the same colour as the walls: Green!

"Come on, let's go and see what mother wants. Someone probably spilled something and without most of the servants here, she'll not know what to do with herself. We'll go and find Star afterwards, and she can have a go at taming your hair." Sorrel put a protective arm around me and led me upstairs.

***

"My daughter is missing, and you have the audacity to tell me that the servants won't be here for another hour to help look for her?" The bellowing voice floated along the corridor, long before we saw whom it belonged to. Tree showed us into the parlour where my mother, almost in tears, was being shouted at by a large woman.

"Ah." A small, harassed smile broke out on her face. "Thank goodness, you are here girls. There's been a bit of an incident."

"A bit of an incident?" the woman roared. "My youngest child has been kidnapped from your castle, and you are calling it a bit of an incident?"

"Now, now, we don't know that she's been kidnapped. She could be hiding somewhere," my mother replied, a hint of panic in her voice. She looked towards Sorrel and me for help.

"We will be happy to help look for her," Sorrel said nicely.

"You'd better be. I've already sent your brothers and sisters out to find her. I swear, if she isn't brought back to me within the hour, I'll..."

"Are your other children involved in the search?" I asked, cutting her off. I figured it would help to know where everyone was looking so Sorrel and I could search somewhere different.

"My children are not servants nor will they perform servant duties. They are getting ready for the meeting later."

"Maybe we would find your daughter faster if we got everyone involved," I said, pointing out, what I thought was an obvious thing to say. Behind the Queen of Hearts, my mother waved her hands and shook her head at me in a panic.

"How dare you!" The large Queen came over to me. At four foot six, I was tiny next to her. I barely came up to her bosom, which would have been right in my face had she not bent over to talk to me. She wiggled a fat finger at me. "I will not have a runt like you telling me how to conduct my family when your own is a pathetic excuse for royalty. I only came here in the vain hope that we could finally come to an agreement on a trade for your water, but since being here in this sorry excuse for a castle, my daughter has been kidnapped, no doubt, by one of your subjects."

She spat out that last word in the same way she might have said troll poo, and by the look on her face as she looked at Tree, she probably rated troll poo higher than The Clubs.

"I don't see how you can call us pathetic when you are the one who can't look after her own children!" I said to the monstrous witch. Her face turned so red that I wondered if steam would come out of her ears.

My mother put her head in her hands, and Sorrel grabbed my arm.

"We'll be happy to join the search," smiled Sorrel as she dragged me out of the room. I could still hear the Queen of Hearts ranting all the way along the corridor.

"What did you drag me away for?" I asked indignantly.

"You don't argue with the Queen of Hearts!" Sorrel replied simply.

"But she was being rude. Did you see Mother? She'd been crying, and nothing makes Mother cry." It was true. Mother ruled our household with an iron fist. I could count on one hand the number of times I'd ever seen her shed a tear.

"I saw, but relations between the four Kingdoms are brittle, and you heard what father told us yesterday. We have got to do our best to accommodate the other royal families and be nice to them. We have to try to forge strong relationships with these people to allow for trade and keep the peace.

"The only thing I want to forge is a sword, and I know that first place I'd stick it. If she thinks Father will trade our water with her after how disgusting she was with Mother, she's got another thing coming!"

"Unfortunately, the magical water of our land is all we have to trade. We've managed to keep hold of it for generations, but, unless father finds something else to trade with, we are probably going to have to give her what she wants."

"You can give her what she wants if you like," I replied in a huff, "but I'm going to wash this newspaper print off my face. It's bad enough that the fat old crow is in the castle, but I don't want to walk around with her on my face too."

And with that, I stalked back to my room and slammed the door. After a few moments of stomping around, I decided that I really should sort my face out and put on a new dress. The party the night before had been a more informal gathering, a chance for the elder royals to reacquaint themselves with each other and for the younger royals to meet each other. Today was the important day. It would kick off in less than an hour with a huge banquet to formally welcome the other royal families. Then the younger royals would leave whilst the oldies talked business.

There was a knock at my door.

"I'm not coming out Sorrel. Go look for her yourself!" I immediately felt bad about being rude to my sister so I opened the door. It was not Sorrel before me, but Star, my next eldest sibling.

"Oh, hey, sorry. I thought you were someone else."

"Evidently. What's Sorrel done?"

"Oh, nothing," I replied, ushering her into the room. "I'm just in a bad mood because the Queen of Hearts screamed at me and I was taking it out on Sorrel."

"Oh," Star moved her face closer to mine and scrunched up her nose before she broke into a huge grin, then started to laugh.

"Why do you have a picture of the Queen of Hearts on your face with the word "ass"' above it?" she giggled.

I looked into my mirror to see what she was talking about. She was right. There was no denying the fact that I'd spent the morning walking around the castle with the word 'ass' printed onto my face accompanied by a picture of the Queen. The headline had originally read "The Royal Hearts travel first class to Clubland", but somewhere along the line, most of it had smudged off leaving only three letters above the photo. It now read "ass". Thank goodness, it had printed backwards so the Queen, herself, had not noticed.

I began to laugh too.

"I'm not surprised she shouted at you. I think I would have done too!" said Star between guffaws.

"She didn't notice the picture. She was shouting at me because I implied she's an incompetent mother."

"You didn't!" Star looked momentarily shocked, then fell over onto the bed with laughter.

"She's lost one of her kids. I thought you'd be out looking for her to be honest. She's got everyone else involved in the search."

"I've just come in from the stables," she said beginning to work on my face, getting me ready for the banquet. She expertly cleansed my face, getting rid of any remnants of newspaper print, despite my protestations. I thought it would be funny to have the Queen's ass on my face. Just as she had done the night before, she tried to get me to wear makeup, which I flatly refused.

"You are a princess! You should wear makeup in public," she implored. She, herself, had little butterfly wings expertly painted around her eyes. It was her signature look. Our other sisters, she had no doubt painted with their flower namesakes.

"I honestly don't know why our parents called you Rose if you won't let me paint them on your face." She folded her arms, which meant I was in for a battle.

"They didn't know when I was born that I wouldn't want flowers all over my face," I retorted with logic.

"You should have been called bog or something!" Star huffed and began to pack away the myriad of makeup brushes she'd been getting out.

"You'd only have wanted to cover me in brown paint if I had," I grinned, but she didn't think I was being funny. "Ok, you can paint a rose on my cheek, but only a tiny one." It was better to give in and let her have her way, and a small rose wasn't so bad. In our kingdom, the girls often wore flowers or some other aspect of nature painted on their faces, usually, whatever they were named after. The Clubs were traditionally named after something from nature, and our parents had gone with plants for my siblings and me. It could have been worse. One of the courtiers was called Stool after the first thing of nature his mother saw after the birth. I don't think she was talking about a chair either.

When she had finished, she looked down at my dress, and her hands flew up to her mouth in shock.

"What did you do?"

I felt bad. Star had hand sewn all our dresses and in an effort to make me look more feminine, had embroidered little roses intertwined with the symbol of our country, the black club, all around the hem.

"Red wine," I replied, bowing my head in shame.

"I'll get you something of mine to wear," she said, running from the room as if my wearing something covered in wine was a threat to everything holy in the world.

Whilst I waited, I decided to look outside into the gardens. Whilst, the Queen of Hearts had been right about the state of our castle, nothing rivalled the breath-taking beauty of the gardens. Even in winter when the trees are leafless, and the flowers are yet to appear, there is still an abundance of evergreens from the pine forest that runs along the outside of the back garden wall to the holly trees, bountiful with red berries. I could see the castle staff scouring the garden, no doubt, for the Queen's lost daughter. The Queen, herself, stood below one of the few trees still in leaf, and though I couldn't hear her from this distance, could tell from the way she stood that she was barking orders at everyone. If she had only bothered to glance upwards, she'd see what I saw now--a little girl in a yellow dress hiding in a tree, and from what I could see, giggling at the furor below her. What an imp!

"This is what I wore last year." Star's voice came from the door behind me. I turned to see her with a small pink dress. You are bigger than me, so it will be very tight on you, but it's all I have that's suitable," she sniffed. I could tell that lending me her own dress was a big deal. I took it gratefully and, after pulling the stained dress off, pulled it over my head. I hate pink, but beggars can't be choosers.

After giving Star a quick kiss on the cheek, I thought it only fair to go down and tell The Queen of Hearts exactly where her daughter was.

I marched across the hard frozen ground to the Queen. A member of staff, Slate, whom I liked and respected very much was now cowering under the glare of the fat old shrew.

"And if you don't find her and bring her back to me this instant, I'll speak to your superiors and make sure you are fired!" She then turned to me. "What do you want? I hope you've come back to apologise for the arrogance and disgraceful behaviour shown earlier."

"I have, your highness," I said and curtseyed. I think it took her by surprise. A smile parted her hideous face.

Out of the corner of my eye, I could see my father approaching, so I knew I'd have to be quick.

"Slate, I apologise for this odious woman's behaviour to you." Slate pulled his head up, a look of horror on his face. It was nothing compared to the expression on the face of the Queen.

"If she had spent more time actually paying attention to her own offspring rather than belittling and shouting at other people, she'd have noticed that her daughter is sitting not fifteen feet above her."

Both The Queen and Slate looked upwards which gave me my chance to escape. I walked quickly in the direction of the castle, right past my father, who asked if everything was all right as I passed. The last thing I heard before the Queen erupted was the sound of giggles coming from the top of the tree.

As the banquet was just about to start, The Queen didn't have enough time to try to ban me from the event. I lined up along with my brothers and sisters in the huge banquet hall ready to be formally introduced to the other royals. I didn't dare look to my left to see the expression on my parents' faces. I knew I was going to be in huge trouble later.

Unfortunately, 'later' came sooner than I thought. The Hearts were the first to be introduced. Even though knew I had to calm myself down, just the thought of her speaking to the staff in that way made me feel angry. Monsatsu only knows what she said to make my mother cry earlier. As the youngest and lowest of The Clubs, I was the first member of my family in the greeting line. It was also the first time I'd been allowed to come, as it was royal decree that no one below the age of fifteen could attend the most important date on the calendar. I'd turned fifteen the past summer, and so I was now allowed to meet the other Kings and Queens formally. The Kings, Queens, and Jacks of the other ruling families would all walk past me, making their way along the line of my family until they were greeted by my own parents and Sage as they stood by the long table that had been set for forty-eight people.

I bowed my head, willing The Queen to say something, anything, despite myself. It would have not taken much for me to really lash out at her. My fists were balled tightly. Star knew my temper and seeing that I was only going to get myself into more trouble, took my left hand and held it tightly in hers.

The Queen, however, was silent and only scowled as my name was read out by Tree, who was the official announcer on occasions like this.

"Lady Rose Persimmon Club."

"Your Highness." I curtsied, no doubt reminding her of the last time I'd curtsied to her in the garden, not half an hour earlier.

"Lady Stargazer Lily Club." Tree called out Star's full name. The King and Queen moved down the line, and I breathed out, releasing the tension in my hands but adding tension to the very tight dress. One of the buttons on the front of Star's dress popped off, making a tiny tinkling sound as it hit the stone floor.

Next to come were the King and Queen of Spades. The Queen glided past me, gracefully, with her feline beauty, and the King plodded behind like a faithful puppy. The two of them had to be the strangest pairing in the history of Vanatus, but they had stood the test of time and had remained married since way before I was born.

The King and Queen of Diamonds came next. The Queen of Diamonds completely ignored my curtsey, protocol, and general manners, and hugged me tightly before moving on to Star and doing the same to her.

I bit back a grin. I liked the Queen of Diamonds. I actually liked all the Diamonds, the richest family in the realm. They were also the most frivolous and fun-loving and had a general zest for life and disregard of the rules. Even now, as I looked, the Queen of Hearts was muttering something under her breath and looking out through sooty eyelashes in a disdainful way. The Queen of Diamonds seemed not to notice that icy daggers were metaphorically hurling their way towards her in the form of the Queen of Hearts icy stare. I delighted in the fact that there was nothing she could do about it, not if she wanted her Kingdom to keep on being supplied by the huge Diamond mines that populated the Diamonds Realm. At least, she'd reserved some of her vitriol for someone that wasn't me.

The Jacks were the next to walk the line. Again, the first was The Jack of Hearts. The Jack was actually the name given to the eldest child of each King and Queen and therefore could be male or female. They came in the same order as their parents, the Jack of Hearts being first. I was surprised when the beauty with whom Tarragon had spent the night came up to me. She'd lied when she'd said she was The Eight of Hearts. She must have known that she'd get found out, but as she walked past me, she gave an almost imperceptible wink, proving that she didn't really care. I desperately wanted to look down the line to see the reaction on Tarragon's face, but it would have meant moving out of position so I had to content myself with imagining it. The Jack of Spades was next. I bent my knees to curtsey, but he took my hand and shook it instead. Unlike the rest of the families, the spades looked vastly different from each other. There was no family resemblance running through them at all, but I knew it was because of their race. Each ruling family in Vanatus was actually the head of a completely different race of beings, and each had their own magic. The Diamonds were not only the richest but were also the bearers of the most magic, sorcerers, magicians, wizards. These were some of the names given to describe them. Their magic was nothing compared to the four founding Aces who were the real mages of Vanatus, but they knew enough to get through life without having to do much beyond flicking a wand every now and again. The Spades were what you might call shifters, each one taking on the ability to turn into an animal or other being at the drop of a hat. There had been a rumour that the royal family were actually multi-shifters, which meant they could change into any number of beings. Such power was extremely rare, though, and the rumour had never been substantiated.

"Good Morning. How are you? I'm Leo."

I was still in shock for a moment. No one had told me that I would have to speak with these people. I'd been told to curtsey and stay quiet, and I was all right with that. I'm not sure my mother had trusted me to actually speak to anyone.

I looked up at him. He was huge with a shaggy mane and amber eyes. There were no prizes for guessing what his shifter animal was.

I suddenly felt shy, and as I was wont to do in situations that made me nervous, I made a complete fool of myself. Instead of saying something along the lines of, "I'm very well M'lord, and yourself?" I instead uttered something I would feel embarrassed about for the rest of the day.

"How are you a lion if your mother is a cat and your father is a dog?"

Star elbowed me in the ribs, but Leo burst out laughing.

"The Queen is a leopard, and my father a wolf," he wheezed between guffaws. "Goodness me, don't let them catch you calling them a cat and a dog. The animal you turn into has no bearing on what your children will turn into. I suppose if my parents had both been panthers for example, my siblings and I would have had a greater likelihood of becoming a panther, too, but as you noticed yourself, my parent's pairing is unusual. All my siblings are different."

"Oh!" I replied for want of anything else to say, and I knew I'd put my foot in it big time. Thank goodness, I was at the opposite end of the line to my parents and the higher royals, and none of them heard my faux pas. I was in enough trouble as it was without adding 'insulting yet another Queen' to the list. Leo moved on to Star who shook his hand and gave a much more respectable answer to his questions.

The Jack of Diamonds was next. She was a tall blonde woman with staggering beauty. Adorned in the diamonds of her home, she simply sparkled. Unlike Leo, she didn't stop to talk to me, but she did give me a warm smile as she passed. Now that all the high royals had gone past, I was free to look to my left.

I could see that the Jack of Diamonds had had to stop as Leo was chatting to every one of my brothers and sisters. I heard the words 'cat and dog' and inwardly cringed. My very first foray into royal life, and I'd already managed to fuck it up. The higher members of the royal families had been coming together like this for years, so they all knew each other, but for me, this was the first time meeting most of them. I looked at the dynamics between the four ruling families. The Queen of Diamonds was laughing away at something that Leo had said whilst the Queen of Hearts stood back and looked on contemptuously at everyone. The King and Queen of Spades were chatting to my father, and the Jack of Hearts was flirting with my second eldest brother, Sequoia, The Ten of Clubs.

I just managed to see the look of jealousy on Tarragon's face before we were all called to dinner.

The lesser royals of each family were brought in to fill up the remaining seats, but, much to my relief, they didn't have to be formally greeted. As we sat, I thought back to how our families came about.

The four ancient mages that ruled the whole of Vanatus decreed millennia ago that each one would have a corner of the Kingdom to rule their own kind. The most powerful, chose the mountainous North East Corner as it held all the diamond mines beneath the snowy peaks and thus he named himself The Ace of Diamonds. The next to choose was the only woman of the group. She chose the flatlands, knowing that it would be a good place to build a city, and following the first Mage's lead christened herself The Ace of Hearts. The third now had the choice between the boggy wetlands and the wild plains and jungles to the northwest. It was an easy choice. For someone like him, a Jaguar Shifter, the heat and plentiful wildlife would be a blessing. He agreed to send some of his people to the mountains to work in the Diamond mines in exchange for some of the profits and thus became The Ace of Spades. The fourth Mage, a squat chap with pointed ears and the least powerful, accepted his plot of land. The marshlands were plentiful in bounty of a different kind, and he secretly thought he'd got the best deal. The clear river that ran through the area teemed with fish and its crystal clear water held its own magical properties. The fruit trees were bountiful and even though there was not a lot of land that was dry enough to be built on, he still thought of it as home from the first second he set eyes on it. His people would survive by hunting, just as he had, and it was his weapon of choice that he coined as his own moniker, The Ace of Clubs.

Time wore on, and the four mages grew old. After many years of ruling, they decided to move out of their respective castles and build one giant one in the centre of Vanatus where the four realms came together. A city was built around it, and here, the four races came together to live, shop, sell and whatever else people did when living in confined spaces. Unfortunately, discord among the groups grew, and the Mages were now too old to put out every fire, so they decreed that they would each pick a family to rule. After a while, it became apparent that the Shifter Royal Family of The Spades had more children than the other races and, therefore, so many royals to keep up with that the mages had to meet once again. A cap was placed upon each family for the number of children the King and Queen of each were allowed to have. The mages agreed that the eldest child would be the heir to the throne, whether male or female, and there could be nine more children. The Spades argued against it, saying that it was quite common for a shifter mother to give birth to a whole litter of pups in one go, whilst the other clans wondered just how on earth they were going to keep up. All these hundreds of years later, the royal families still kept to the tradition of having ten children each. Kings only chose healthy brides, up to the task of rearing so many children, whilst the female Jacks who were born to the position, secretly prayed that the rule would be abolished before they came to power and, until then, kept their legs crossed. Unfortunately for The Spades, It was difficult to plan the exact number of children when whole litters could be upwards of six or seven. The Queen of Spades had given birth to exactly seventeen children, but because of the law, only the elder eleven could be called royal. The younger ones were still her children, though, and so they had been deposited in one of the palace bedrooms with a couple of nanny goat shifters to look after them. There were also a couple of younger Heart royals up there too. I wasn't sure why The Queen of Hearts had gone over the limit, but judging by the way she was, perhaps she didn't like to be beaten in anything, and that meant childbirth too. The law was ancient and draconian, and the thought of having eleven children made me wince. As the Two of Clubs, no one cared one jot if I had any children, which was fine by me as I fully intended to become a warrior. Warriors, as a general rule, didn't just stop mid-war and give birth.

I looked around the table in awe of the people around me. These were the most powerful people in the whole of Vanatus if you didn't count the Aces. If someone decided to catapult flaming boulders at the castle or find some other way to flatten it, the whole of Vanatus would be left with no members of royalty at all.

"I can't believe you said that about The King and Queen of Spades!" Star nudged me. "And you've got your hair in your soup."

I groaned. The soggy, tomatoey hair, I could deal with, but my mighty faux pas was still causing me to cringe inwardly.

"I didn't mean to, but look at them. They look so weird together."

The Queen of Spades was busy licking the soup daintily straight from the bowl without the aid of a spoon, whilst her husband was sniffing it with a delighted look on his face. Leo caught my eye and winked causing me to blush the same colour as the soup. At the other side of the table, a couple of the younger Diamonds were casting spells at each other under the table. I only knew because I saw a telltale flash of purple and the youngest of the two now had bushier eyebrows than he had before. I made a mental note to stay out of their way later. I didn't want to end up with blue hair or some other magical mishap.

At the end of the meal, all the royal children would be expected to leave, barring the Jacks who would stay with their parents to discuss the running of the four Kingdoms and how to keep peace among them. Judging by the look The Queen of Hearts was giving The Queen of Diamonds, they'd struggle to keep peace amongst themselves, let alone amongst their respective subjects.

However, the end of the meal was at least five courses away, and I was already beginning to feel queasy. The soup churned in my stomach and threatened to make a reappearance. My first foray into alcohol was now coming back to haunt me. When the servants brought out the next course, flambéed swamp fish in apple and toadspawn sauce, a Club delicacy, my stomach heaved, and I had to excuse herself quickly so as not to cause a scene by throwing up my starter. I'd embarrassed myself too much in the past hour to add puking up dinner to the list of stupid things I'd done that day.

"Crud," I said, kicking the toilet moments later and feeling very ashamed into the process. I added a painful toe into the mix of everything that had gone wrong and proceeded to throw up again. "Crud, crud, crud!"

Skipping the rest of dinner entirely, I decided to go down to my favourite place in the gardens and worry about my father's wrath later. I'd tell him I was too ill to eat, which was the honest truth. With some luck, the Queen of Hearts might be so carried away with hating The Queen of Diamonds that she'd neglect to tell my parents what I said to her. The bitterly fresh air hit me as I exited the castle, making me feel instantly better and more refreshed. I pulled out my leather armour, sword, and shield from my secret hidey-hole and kitted myself up.

My eldest brothers had the luxury of a training square with targets, choice of weapons, and the best warfare trainers that Club money could buy, but as the youngest member of the royal family and a girl to boot, I was not allowed to go inside it. Sage had taken me inside once when he'd finally got sick of my begging, only to have been scolded by our mother. I had been grounded inside the castle for a week as punishment.

Sage later brought me a sword.. It was a training sword and so wasn't very pretty, but a sword is a sword, and an ugly sword can inflict as much damage as a beautiful one. The shield, made out of wood with leather straps, and the armour, I'd made myself.

I quickly took myself to the only part of the garden that was invisible to anyone looking out of the castle windows, a spot behind a huge hedgerow, which I considered my spot, and began to swing the sword, pretending The Queen of Hearts was in front of me.

I didn't know the correct terms for the moves I was making, but I'd seen my brothers practicing them often enough to know I was doing it right. It's not like, knowing the names of them would exactly help me in the first place right? An enemy isn't going to be any less dead if I knew the name of the move that killed him. I loved the weight of the sword in my hand, the precision of my movements and the feel of the leather against my skin. I felt more at home out here being a secret warrior than I did inside being a real princess. I just had to be careful not to mess up the pretty dress that Star had lent me. My mother would pitch a fit if she saw me now, but she was in the banquet hall with the other royals. If I played it right, I could get a good hour of practice in before going back to the castle and re-joining the others for dessert.

The air was frigid and the ground hard as nails. That was good because it meant that there was less chance of getting my dress muddied up. I could see my breath as I twirled, throwing my sword around me, defeating unseen foes and beheading imaginary monsters. The truth was, I had more drive to be a warrior than any of my brothers even though it was something that was expected of them. All that was expected of me was to curtsey at foreign dignitaries and try to stay clean. It was so unfair! Tarragon was allowed to be inducted into warrior training, and he could barely hold a knife and fork without needing help. It drove me mad, but I channelled my anger at the injustice by practicing harder, becoming more skilled. My sword whipped through the air, almost invisible in its speed. Had any foe been nearby, they would surely have thought twice about attacking me and woe betide the Queen of Hearts coming anywhere near me now whilst I was in the zone. She would have her ugly head hitting the floor before she had enough time to open her mouth. Not that there was much chance of her coming out to see if I was all right. I guess I wasn't her favourite person at the moment either. As it was, there was only a doe with her fawn watching me lazily from the other side of the garden.

Something in the air shifted which caused me to quiet my sword. The Doe, startled by a noise, fled into the wooded area on the very far side of the garden, followed quickly by the lolloping fawn.

I didn't have the nose of the shifting Spades but even I knew there was something wrong. A noise of flapping wings came from the direction of the swamps to my left. I'd only heard it a couple of times in my life, both of which had been preceded by my mother pulling me into the castle as quickly as she could and then locking all the doors behind her. My instincts told me to run from the noise, but I already knew I wouldn't be quick enough. The flapping noise was getting stronger, and it would come over the garden wall within seconds. I ran around the huge bush that shielded me from the view of the castle and began to run as fast as my legs would carry me toward the castle. Looking over my shoulder, I saw the huge red dragon emerge. He looked like an angry bastard, and any hope that I had of the dragon just flying overhead left me. I was no dragon expert, but it was plain to see that this one was hungry. The awkward armour I had fashioned for myself slowed me down. I'd spent so much time practicing with the sword that I'd given myself no time to practice the fine art of running away from danger. Stupidly thinking I'd always be brave enough to handle anything, running away had not factored highly on my self-imposed training schedule. I'd not brought dragons into the equation, though, an oversight on my part. I was so caught up in looking to see if the dragon was gaining on me that I didn't notice the rock in front of me, and I went tumbling over myself, snapping my shield in two in the process. I knew that getting up and running was not an option now. My only course of action would be to turn over and face the hungry beast. The chances of me surviving were slim, but I still had my sword. If I thrust it upwards in just the right place as the dragon came to take me, I might just make it. It was the longest of long shots, and if the dragon decided to barbeque me first, the whole thing would be a moot point anyway. I pulled back my arm ready to strike, but the dragon sailed right over me as though I wasn't even there. The Clubs were blessed with very little magic, and the tiny bit we did possess had mainly to do with healing. We were also great at growing things and working with nature, none of which would help me in the situation I was in, so why had the dragon ignored me? He certainly looked hungry. And then I saw it. The Spade children stood looking excitedly out of the tower window with their ignorant nanny pointing at the dragon. Did the goat shifter not know about dragons at all?

"Close the window!" I shouted, waving my hands and running towards the castle, but it was already too late. I could see the small children, two or three of them, in the talons of the dragon as he lifted his wings and once again flew over the castle ramparts. The Nanny screamed and closed the window, but it was too late now. The damage had already been done.

I panicked. Dragons almost never came close to civilisation. They preferred to stay up in the mountains and eat goats and other mountain animals. It would take me too long to go back in the castle and alert the people inside. I imagined the scream of the nanny would have them all racing up to the tower anyway where they would find a frightened nanny and three missing children. There was only one person who was close enough to follow the dragon before it got away and I was that person.

Following on foot wasn't an option, so I ran through a sidewall of the castle grounds where I knew that the visiting royals would have parked their vehicles. The Clubs' main method of transportation was their own feet but to carry heavy loads or travel long distances, my parents had a stable of shire horses. I loved every one of those horses, but they weren't up to the job of racing after a dragon. I surveyed the rest of what was available to me. The Hearts had come in a variety of mechanical wheeled and winged machines that looked amazing, but as I had never driven so much as a go-cart in my life, I wouldn't know how to begin to operate one. The Diamonds had arrived on a fleet of Arabian horses and palominos, the shiny muscled Arabians for the menfolk and the stunning white palominos with long flowing hair for the ladies. Honestly, were horses supposed to look that pretty? The Spades, on the other hand, had brought with them a whole host of creatures. Some of the Spades would be able to get there under their own steam. I knew for a fact that the Seven and Eight of Spades were bird shifters. An eagle and an owl, specifically, but the others would have to find other ways to get here, hence the various winged beasts. A stunning winged unicorn looked like my safest bet, as some of the others animals had sharp teeth. Considering I had never encountered such creatures before, it seemed wise to steer clear of them. I hoisted myself onto the unicorn's back not having ridden any kind of horse beyond our old Shires, let alone a horned, winged one. I grabbed hold of its mane and slapped it hard on the rump. The Unicorn brayed, pulling itself up onto just its hind legs, nearly causing me to fall off, but then it began a run and spread its magnificent wings, and before I knew it, we were airborn.

Being a Club, flying was not something I was either familiar or comfortable with. If Monsatsu had made us to fly, he would have given us wings. Even though my thoughts on flying were already that it was unnatural, I was completely unprepared for the thrill of fear that now ran through me as the ground beneath me got smaller and smaller. What a time to develop a fear of heights. I grabbed hold of the unicorn's mane tighter and decided the best way not to have a complete meltdown was to focus on the reason I was up here in the first place. I scanned the sky for the dragon; it had disappeared completely. How was that possible? He'd not got that much of a head start. It was only when I heard a distant shriek that I realised I'd been looking in completely the wrong direction. The dragon had not gone back to the swamplands from which it had come, but had instead headed towards the huge walled city of the capital of Vanatus, Urbis, in which the four Aces lived, and the Kings and Queens of each kingdom conducted their affairs of state, each with their own corner of the city.

This, in itself, was strange for so many reasons. I'd not thought of it when I first saw the dragon. I was too busy fearing for my life, but dragons don't live in the swamps. There is a dragon colony in the distant mountains, but they almost never come into civilisation. The fact that the dragon had now headed for Urbis was surprising. This was clearly no ordinary dragon.

I geed up the unicorn who huffed at being ridden so hard and by someone so inexperienced.

"I promise to give you a carrot if you go faster, catch up with the dragon, and get us all back to the ground safely," I said. If he got the children and me home in one piece, he could have a whole field of carrots as far as I was concerned.

We were up in the air for hours, the dragon and the unicorn equally matched for speed. Part of me wanted to get close enough to the dragon to end it, but another part of me knew that I didn't have any kind of coherent plan. A fight with a dragon would be difficult on the ground, but one in the air? It would be deadly. I still had the three children to consider. Looking out across the sky, I could see them now. There were definitely three children, and they were all very young judging by the size of them, although it was sometimes difficult to tell with shifters. Fully grown bunny Spades tended to be tiny people. From this distance, it was still impossible to tell if they were Spade children or Hearts, which was the only other royal family with younger children at the castle. The Diamonds youngest child was nineteen, and my own mother had given up having children when I was born, saying her duty as Queen was done, and as I was such a handful, she couldn't possibly do it all again. Of course, this was said in jest, or at least, I hoped it was.

Obviously, whichever suit's children were taken, it would be bad news. But if one of them happened to be a Heart, well, the consequences didn't bear thinking about. Relations between the Clubs and the Hearts were strained, at best, and I didn't think that having their youngest kidnapped right from the Club castle tower was going to improve things. Especially, since said child had already disappeared once today.

The unicorn was beginning to huff and puff a lot more now, and a slick sheen of sweat covered its perfect white body. It was beginning to flag under the strain. The bright lights of Urbis on the horizon and the unique silhouette of the Aces' castle loomed ever closer. Four huge white towers with spires rising up majestically in the centre of the huge city dominated the skyline.

"Why is the dragon heading for Urbis?" I wondered aloud. The unicorn grunted in answer. Having three of the royal children was bad enough, but if he got as far as the walled city with its tens of thousands of inhabitants, it could wreak havoc on the whole of the four lands. I slapped my legs on the side of the unicorn and shouted at him to hurry up. I'd owe the beast a whole cartful of carrots, the way things were shaping up.

The unicorn, sensing my urgency, gave a final burst of speed, and for the first time since setting off, the dragon finally noticed that it was being followed. It curled its head towards us and gave a blast of fire, taking me by surprise. It missed its mark, but it was close enough to scorch the unicorn's wingtip and make it hesitate.

"Come on, boy, you can do it," I shouted, urging the tired equine on. I knew he wouldn't understand the Vanatusian language that all the races spoke, but I hoped he'd understand the message by the tone of my voice.

He seemed to understand the spirit of the message as he flapped his wings harder. The dragon tried again to hit us with fire, but we were ready. We ducked to the side, missing the flames by a good few feet. The dragon was really angry now. It was obviously on a mission, and we were getting in its way. It tried again to shoot flames at us, missing again but with less distance than before. I actually began to think I could battle this creature now, but I had to be careful, he was still holding the children. As if he'd magically understood my thoughts, he let go of one of the children, and I watched in horror as it tumbled toward the ground. I had only one choice to make. I had to leave the dragon and save the child. Kicking my legs, I pulled the mane in a way I hoped would make the unicorn understand meant to go down. Luckily, the unicorn had more experience with flying than I and pushed its head down into a steep dive. I tried not to think about the ground coming up at me with considerable speed, and instead, concentrated on the tiny figure falling below me. In a panic, it had shifted into its animal form, making it even smaller and harder to see.

'Why couldn't it be some kind of bird shifter?' I thought to myself as I willed the unicorn to go faster. The tiny animal was so difficult to see, so it's couldn't have been a rhino, or an elephant shifter. On further thought, this was probably for the best as I wasn't sure if a unicorn could hold a rhino, even a small one.

The unicorn put on one more big burst of speed, and I reached out and caught the cub by the scruff of its neck just as the unicorn pulled up and came in to land in a poppy-strewn meadow.

The thing in my hand trembled, and as I looked down, the red hair and distinctive pointed face told me the little cub was actually a fox cub. I shielded my eyes against the setting sun and saw the silhouette of the dragon, still with the other two children, now just a small black speck on the horizon. I watched as it dipped lower, right over the walls of Urbis.

The unicorn nodded its head down and began to munch on some of the poppy heads so I jumped off, keeping the fox cub safely in my arms. I heard the distinctive sound of a brook cutting through the overgrown meadow, which made sense. Poppies wouldn't bloom in the middle of winter anywhere but The Clublands and only then when near a source of magical water. Leading the unicorn to it, I sat on the small bank and plunged my hands into the crystal clear water. We were still in Club territory, I could tell that by the magical properties of the water, but I could see the plains of the Spadelands to my right. The little cub licked the drips of water from my cupped hand and then began to tremble. At first, I thought it was because of fear, but then I realised it was the telltale sign of a shifter turning back to its human form. I placed it carefully on the bank and turned my attention to the water, which I drank down greedily. The residual effect of the morning's hangover was still thudding through my temples. Star had told me, only yesterday, that the only real cure for a hangover was to keep hydrated, eat a greasy breakfast, and do some exercise. The only one of those I'd managed was the exercise part, and I suspected that Star hadn't quite meant chasing a dragon as a form of exercise.

I drank down as much of the delicious water as I could and only stopped when I heard a small voice beside me.

"Hello," the fox cub turned out to be a very cute little Spade girl with straight auburn hair and scared golden eyes peeking out from the longest lashes I'd ever seen.

"Hey kid, you ok?" It was a stupid question. The poor kid was completely naked in the middle of a meadow in winter, after being dropped out of the sky by a fire-breathing dragon. Her clothes must have fallen from her as she changed. I scoured the land around me for any sight of them but if they had fallen in the field at all, they were hidden by the poppies that grew here.

"I'm cold." She began to shiver which had nothing to do with shifting.

"I think you should turn back into your fox form. At least that way, you'll have a natural fur coat on."

"I can't, it takes a lot of magic to turn, and I've used it all up. I need to rest or have some sningleberries."

I wasn't familiar with sningleberries. They must have been a plant indigenous to the Spadelands. I wanted to ask exactly what one was and where to find it, but the poor kid was turning blue. I pulled off my leather armour and the tunic that I'd thrown over Star's party dress to keep it clean. I passed the tunic to the girl and pulled my armour back on. With a groan, I noticed that the very ends of the handmade dress had been singed and were now black instead of the pastel pink colour of the rest of the dress. Not that I cared about dresses, but I felt awful at ruining another of Star's dresses, and this was more than definitely ruined. The bottom of the dress was now a charred black mess. There was an acrid burning smell emanating from it.

"Well, that's had it," I said to myself wearily.

"What is?" asked the little girl. The tunic, which had been pretty short on me, completely covered the little girl and dragged along the ground.

"Nevermind. Who else did the dragon take?" I prayed that the name Heart didn't come up.

"Lepu and Lucy."

I didn't recognise the names, but I knew Lucy wasn't a shifter name. It sounded human, which meant only one thing. "Was Lucy a Heart?"

"Yes. Lepu is my brother."

I scanned through my knowledge of shifters. They tended to name their offspring something that had something to do with their shifter animal. "Lepu, he's a hare right?"

"Yes!" The young girl's eyes grew wide. She was obviously not expecting a Club to know anything about Spades.

"And you must be...Vulpa?" I hazarded a guess.

"Vulpina." Close but no cigar.

I looked back to the unicorn, who had had his fill of the water and had gone back to chewing on flowers.

"Ok, Vulpina, we have two choices. Either we take you back to your parents at my castle and tell them where the dragon took your brother, or we get back on this unicorn and go get them."

I knew that going back to the castle would probably mean certain death for Lepu and Lucy, but to chase the dragon would put little Vulpina back in harm's way. Maybe taking her back would be the best option? It was possible that there were dragon fighters in Urbis, people much more skilled than I could ever hope to be. Maybe some of them would not have hangovers. Yes, leaving the decision to the scared little child was a good idea. That way, we could go back to the castle, knowing I had tried my best and had, at least managed to save one of the royal kids. What I wasn't expecting was the spunky nature of Vulpina, who had pulled herself up to her full height (which wasn't much) and stuck out her scrawny chest.

"We need to go and rescue my brother. He's only five. He needs me to rescue him!"

I sighed. "And how old are you exactly?"

"I'm six!" she replied proudly.

"I thought so." I sighed again. Thank Monsatsu that I'd been wearing my armour when the dragon flew over the garden wall, it looked like I was going to need it.

"Come on, boy," I tried to urge the reluctant unicorn into the air once I'd climbed on with Vulpina in front of me.

He was having none of it, having just found a patch of deliciously juicy grass to munch on.

"I'm sorry, my friend, but we just don't have time for dinner just yet." I guiltily slapped his hind quarters with the flat side of the sword. I, like the rest of the Clubs, was an animal lover, and the last thing I wanted to do was hurt the unicorn, but I had to get to the other children quickly. He let out a very un-horse-like bellow and took off a canter before once again, spreading his wings and soaring into the air. I took the time to fully appreciate the beauty of the ground below me. The fear I had originally felt at being so high in the air had dissipated a little, and now I could enjoy looking out at our lands below, bathed in the soft sunlight of the disappearing winter sun. It was still only early afternoon, but the sun dipped low in the sky. In the summer months, there would be hours of daylight left, but now, I'd have to find the dragon quickly, or I would be flying blind in the winter darkness. A huge light up ahead caught my eye, and I suddenly realised that finding the dragon and flying in the dark, were not going to be problems. At least two parts of the huge metropolis were on fire, and with the abundance of straw roofs in The Club Quarter, it didn't take a genius to realise that a fire could have a huge impact on the people that lived and worked there. As I came to the huge grey stone outer walls, I prayed that the fires were in the Heart quarter where they had brick houses and would be better equipped to deal with it, or the Diamond quadrant where they used strong white stone, mined when the seams had given up their fill of diamonds. The Spades had a mix of houses made from anything they could find so a fire would be catastrophic for them, too. I should have felt bad about wishing a fire on the Hearts and Diamonds, but my only concern was my own people, them and the two missing children.

I heard it before I saw it. Urbis was huge, but the screams coming from inside were undeniable. Vulpina held on tightly as we descended on the edge of the huge city, just outside the massive wrought iron gates. Hundreds of people were running over the drawbridge that cut Urbis off from the rest of the world in times of war. Some fled on horseback, and the air was alive with hundreds of people fleeing on unicorns, griffins, and other winged creatures. The roar of steam-powered motors cut through the noise as the Hearts used their own wheeled and winged contraptions to escape. It was a struggle to walk through the tide of people, but they parted around us, so eventually we were in Urbis itself. To the left, was the Club district and to the right was the fashionable Heart district known as Cerce. A huge pathway cut between both parts of the city, serving as both an unofficial border between the two lands and a road straight to the huge Ace Palace, a building that dominated Urbis. On the left of the wide road was a wall, erected by the Hearts as a way to keep out the riff-raff (i.e. anyone who wasn't a Heart). Although they did let other cultures into their district, they made them walk through a small doorway whilst an extremely fashionable Heart looked down on them as they entered. Literally, the fashion police! It wasn't this part of town that I was interested in, though. The Club Quarter was as open as the Heart District was closed, and it was here that we headed. I threaded my way past little houses and thatched cottages until we came to, what was probably the smallest house in the whole of Urbis. I jumped down from the back of the unicorn, bringing Vulpina with me and knocked on the little wooden door. An old Crone answered, and Vulpina slunk back at the sight of her, hiding behind my legs.

"Vulpina," I said, dragging the little girl out from behind me. "this is Wisteria Blogd. She was my nanny for many years." Vulpina took one look at the old woman and cringed. Wisteria, for her part, cracked a massive grin that showed the only tooth in her mouth.

"Wisty, could you look after Vulpina for me, please? There is a dragon on the loose, and it has some children."

"No!" screamed Vulpina, clutching onto my legs so tightly now that I had to prise her off as one would prise open a mussel. "I wanna come with you!"

"Vulpina, I need to find your brother and Lucy, and I can't risk you getting hurt. Wisteria was the best nanny I ever had, and she'll do a good job of looking after you. I promise to come back for you soon."

I looked at the little cottage's thatched roof. "Wisty, The dragon is in Cerce somewhere, but something is making it angry, and it's blowing fire all over the place. I think it would be best if you take Vulpina and get out of here. I'll meet you on the other side of the outer wall as soon as I can. Thanks for this." I kissed the nanny on the cheek and hopped back onto the unicorn before Vulpina got the chance to follow. One swift kick of my legs and we were once again soaring into the sky.

I could see where the fire was now. Some parts of the Cerce and one of the spires of the Ace's castle were billowing smoke. People were screaming and running around in a mass panic. The problem with trying to keep people out had now become the problem of being unable to get out. The huge wall around Cerce had only a few exits, and I could see bottlenecks forming as people tried desperately to get through them. In the centre of Cerce, a chain had been formed passing buckets of water from one to the next to throw on the burning buildings. I still couldn't see the dragon through the carnage.

Then I heard it. It's distinctive bellowing roar coming from the northern part of the district. Tugging on the unicorn's mane, I guided him through the greyness of the smoke. When we came through the other side, I could see the redness of the dragon. He was not that far in front of me and looked to be on the border between Cerce and Diamas, the Diamond Quarter. He still had the children in his claws! He looked even angrier than he had before, and the precise trails of fire he'd emitted when I was following him had now turned into a frenzy of breathing fireballs at everyone. It was a wonder those children were still alive. Through the smoke, I could just about see what it was that was making him angry. Some of the Diamonds were throwing rocks at him and pointing their wands in an effort to make him drop the children or kill him. Either of which would have surely ended in the death of the little ones. He wasn't that high in the air, but even a fall from thirty feet would kill them. Purple jets of light sliced through the air, almost like a strange lightning. I didn't know what spells the Diamonds were using, but I would bet that the results would be catastrophic if they were to hit the children.

"Stop!" I tried circling round the dragon, giving it enough of a wide berth so that it wouldn't cremate me on the spot and signalled to the Diamonds to stop what they were doing. As I passed over the top of the border that separated the two districts, I saw something that drove fear into my heart. They were loading up a trebuchet with a huge flaming boulder. The flames were purple. Magic!

"No!" I tried signalling the Diamonds again, but over the roar of the dragon and the noise of the people, none of them heard me. The feeling of heat across my back and the feeling of singed hair made me realise that the Dragon itself had noticed what the Diamonds hadn't.

The unicorn gave a cry of pain and flew to the ground in a circle, landing right at the inside edge of Cerce. As I looked behind me, I could see a huge burn mark across the back of the unicorn, now scorched black. Its tail had been practically burnt off and even more alarmingly, the tip of its right wing was still on fire. I threw myself off in a panic and looked about me for some water. The unfamiliar buildings that were distinctive of Cerce surrounded me and made me feel even more uncertain of which way to turn. Alleys seemed to spread out in all direction in the sprawling mass of close-knit buildings in the district. I frantically looked at the signs around me, looking for something that could help. Fashion shops surrounded me, one for just hats and one that had the most ridiculously fancy and impractical shoes filling the window. Nothing that would have water in it. I then spotted a sign advertising The Alchemist House, which judging by the picture, was a cocktail bar. I ran through the doors into the deserted bar. It looked nothing like the alehouses I'd seen in the Club district. Thousands of bottles full of interesting looking liqueurs and mixers lined the wall in a colour-coordinated fashion. A vat of something smoked with dry ice or magic on the bar top. I scanned the bottles for something that would not contain alcohol as throwing that on the flames would only increase them. The problem was, I didn't recognise any of the names printed on the bottles. I finally found a silver bucket of ice, which had partially melted. Picking it up, I ran outside. The unicorn was spinning round in circles in a panic. I timed it perfectly and threw the whole lot over the unicorn's wing. It spluttered out with a hiss. I scrabbled around on the ground where the ice had fallen and picked up as much as I could to place it on the burnt back of the unicorn.

It soothed it slightly, and it stopped its panicked trotting around and let me apply the ice. On closer inspection, I found that the burn was superficial and would heal. A few treatments in the healing water of The Clublands, and it would be as good as new. For now, though, the ice would have to do. There was no denying it, the once stunning white coat and flowing hair were now blackened with soot, and the long tail had been reduced to a black stump. It had lost quite a few feathers on its right wing tip, which even the rivers and streams of the Clublands wouldn't be able to fix but it should still be able to fly.

A roar from above me, followed by a huge thud that sent shock waves around, told me that the Diamonds had started their campaign. A nearby shop had completely disappeared. At first, I thought it had just been levelled with the impact of the boulder, but I now saw that the Diamonds had used magic as both the boulder and shop had literally disappeared--no smoke, no debris, just a hole in the ground where the shop once stood.

Panic filled me. There was no one around on the Heart side of the wall to help me, and I had no way of communicating with the Diamonds.

"Shitty death! Monsatsu, what should I do?" I was not usually one to pray to a deity, but I think that almost being set on fire by a rampaging dragon whilst having magic boulders flung at me was enough of a reason to merit it.

As if the god I didn't believe in had actually heard me, I spotted something that might help. A shop sign further down the street advertised an array of strange machines for which the Hearts were well known. It was a long shot, but if there was anything that could help me, that was the place. Maybe I could find one of those flying bike machine things that The Hearts used as transport.

The shop was full of the most strange and curious objects I'd ever seen. Having only every visited this district on one occasion, the ways of The Hearts were largely foreign to me. I'd occasionally see them on my trips to

The Club quarter of Urbis, but, apart from their four yearly trips to The Club Marshlands, I never saw a Heart. Whilst the Clubs and Spades relied on nature and the Diamonds used magic to get things done, the Hearts were reliant on technology. They used machines for everything from transport to cooking and a lot of the gadgets they had come up with lined the huge shop. Unfortunately, as the shop was so small, space being at a premium in this quarter, there was nothing like the steam-powered transport I'd seen the Royal Hearts in when they showed up to the castle. This place was full of small gadgets, and I had no idea what any of them were used for. The smell of oil filled the air, and the abundance of cogs and levers on everything told me that I'd not know how to work anything even if I knew what it did. Knowing my luck, I'd take a machine out only to find it was a food mixer. Then I saw it. Right at the back of the shop, a sign saying restricted section. If there was going to be anything I needed to get rid of a dragon, that would be the section to find it.

I passed through the door, ignoring the sign that said I had to be eighteen and found myself in a dark room. The Hearts used electricity to power their lights, but back in my own land, we used torches and oil lamps. How did the lights work again? I tried to remember how to turn them on. I'd only seen them used once, and it was a long time ago. It was something to do with the wall. I felt my way along until I came to a button. When I found it, light flooded the room leaving me in awe at its contents. A whole wall was taken up with swords of all different sizes and descriptions from jewel-encrusted daggers to a huge sword, made up of the most intricate metalwork I'd ever seen, obviously goblin forged. Part of me wanted that sword so badly, but despite it being the most magnificent weapon I'd ever laid my eyes on, it was completely useless against a dragon if I couldn't get close enough to it to use the damn thing. No, I needed something that worked from a distance. Along the next wall were various throwing weapons. I would have loved to have a go with those, but I'd not got that far in my training, having only practiced with the sword. I vowed to come back one day and pick out something from that wall. For now, though, it was the guns that interested me. I'd never used one, the Clubs preferred to use the clubs that bore their name, swords, and occasionally, bows and arrows. I would have preferred the latter, but I needed one hand to cling on to the unicorn. The wall of guns both scared me and thrilled me at the same time. Some looked so complicated that I'd need a PhD from the University of Urbis just to turn them on. I picked up the one that looked the least complicated, a medium-sized, brass-coloured thing with one on button and a trigger. It seemed simple enough. I grabbed it, hoping it didn't need to charge up or need some kind of battery. I was woefully lacking in knowledge of how machines worked.

"I'm sorry. I'm going to have to get back on you. I'll try to stay clear of the painful areas." I said to the Unicorn as I got back to where I'd left him. I felt horrible having to use him again, but he seemed to understand. He bent his forelegs so I could jump up easily. I stroked what was left of his mane and once more took off into the air for the final battle with the dragon.

It was now locked in a battle with the Diamonds on the other side of the huge wall. Another boulder flew over the wall, missing the dragon but demolishing the Alchemist bar. I wasn't sure if we were in more danger from the dragon or the Diamonds, who were firing boulders willy-nilly over the wall. Whilst he was paying attention to the Diamonds, I flew up behind him as close as I dared. I pressed the button on the gun, and it began to vibrate alarmingly, almost causing me to drop it. A surge of power radiated up my arm. I knew I was going to have to pull the trigger quickly to discharge it, or I'd drop it. Cursing myself for not picking something smaller, I aimed at the dragon. Instead of the bullets I was expecting, a wall of fire emerged, taking me by surprise and giving the dragon a taste of its own medicine. It gave out an unearthly shriek and began to spin in the sky. I'd got it! Its wing was on fire! I urged the unicorn towards it as it did exactly what I expected. Two little figures dropped through the air, hurtling to the ground. I was ready. The unicorn gave a burst of speed, dodging the flailing dragon, and with just feet to spare, I caught both children.

Placing them on the ground, I gave them a quick once over to make sure they were both ok. By some miracle, they both seemed unscathed. They were terrified, by the look of them, but with no visible cuts and bruises.

"Are you all right?"

Neither child spoke. The one I took to be Lucy cried, whilst Lepu bowed his head and trembled. I recognised Lucy as the imp who had been hiding from her mother in the tree earlier.

"My name is Rose. It was from my castle that you were taken. I flew here on this unicorn to save you. You are safe now." I was no good with little kids, but I did the best I could to comfort them. Lucy remained silently sobbing, but Lepu whispered something.

"Excuse me?" I asked him to repeat what he said.

"Elphin. The unicorn is called Elphin. He belongs to my sister."

"Well, Elphin saved both your lives. He also saved Vulpina. She's safe over in The Club District." I hoped that this little snippet of information would cheer them up, at least, but before they had a chance to respond, an almighty crash rumbled the street around us like an earthquake. It was only when the dragon bounced off the nearest rooftop, almost demolishing the building in its wake, and fell to the ground just around the corner from where we were standing that I realised what the noise was.

"Lucy, Lepu, can you look after Elphin for me?" I figured giving them something to do would take their minds off themselves and keep them from running after me. The last thing I needed was a couple of little kids nearby when I slaughtered the dragon, once and for all.

Feeling around my right-hand side, I drew my sword from its sheath and took off in the direction the dragon had fallen, but when I rounded the corner, it had disappeared. There was only a red-haired man lying on the cobbled ground groaning and clutching his side. I ran to him, dropping to my knees. The dragon had got him, his skin blackened on his arm and side. A flash went off from behind me. Lightening? At least, it had waited until the dragon was floored, but where was he? The street was empty.

"Which way did he go?" I asked the man. His face contorted into a grimace of pain. I was no doctor, but I held out little hope for this man's survival. The magic of the Diamonds might have been able to cure him, but I suspected that he wouldn't even survive long enough to be picked up and put on the back of Elphin, let alone flown over the high wall separating the border between the two districts.

The man let out a groan. I felt completely useless. I knew that bandaging the burnt area wouldn't help, but I couldn't think of anything else to do. My life as a princess meant I was woefully unprepared for the big bad world, and a lack of education in basic first aid was one of my shortfalls. It was something I would remedy at the first available opportunity, but for now, I had nothing.

"You'll be ok," I said, pointlessly. He knew as well as I did that he was a goner unless someone who knew how to deal with third-degree burns turned up pretty quickly.

"Help!" I yelled out, although I already knew there was no one nearby to help. The lightning flashed again as I put my arm under his head and stroked his hair. It was the only thing I felt capable of doing.

"My babies!" The man rasped. I didn't know what he was talking about. Maybe he was delirious with the pain. "Vulpina, Lepu."

He was definitely delirious.

"I don't know what you mean," I replied. He began to try to sit up but groaned with pain. In my panic at watching this man die, I pulled him back.

"Don't move. Someone will come for us." I lied. No one was coming.

"Where are Vulpina and Lepu? Are they ok? I dropped them."

"What? No, the dragon dropped them. I got him, they are safe," in the panic of finding this man, I'd completely forgotten about the dragon. I looked around quickly to make sure that he wasn't nearby. I couldn't see or hear him anymore. He'd slunk off somewhere to either hide or die.

"My babies are safe?"

"Vulpina and Lepu, the Spade children are safe."

"I'm a Spade." I'd thought as much. He didn't have the same air about him as a Heart, and if he had been a Diamond, he could probably have fixed himself with the aid of magic. He had the look of a shifter. With his red colouring, he reminded me a little of Vulpina. Perhaps he was a fox too. Still, now wasn't the right time to enquire

"The Queen...I..." His head lolled to the side, his eyes still open but now unseeing. I tried shaking him to no avail. He was dead. The lightning flashed one more time causing me to gaze skywards. There wasn't a cloud in the sky.

I closed his eyes and laid his head back down on the cobbles below him. There was nothing I could do for him now and nowhere I could take him. The only people I knew to be within the walls of Cerce were Lepu, Lucy, Elphin, and me. It was with a heavy heart that I realised I'd have to leave his body here. I wouldn't be able to fit him on Elphin, not when I had three small children to take back to their parents. I made a mental note to tell the King and Queen of Spades so they could make arrangements to collect his body and take him back to his family if he had any.

The dragon was the next thing on my list to deal with. He'd gone strangely quiet since he'd fallen to the ground. I ran right down to the end of the cobbled street and looked both right and left when I got to a T-junction. He wasn't there. How was it possible to lose a huge injured dragon? There were plenty of small alleyways and hidden passageways in the warren of shops and restaurants, but none were big enough to hide a dragon. I passed the dead man again and went back to join the kids.

By some miracle, both kids, plus the unicorn stood in the same place I'd left them. I scooped the little ones up and put them on Elphin's back, making sure they wouldn't be sitting on his burns, before jumping on myself. I hated making the poor creature fly once again, but I'd never find my way out of the maze that was Cerce if I had to walk.

I landed just outside Wisteria's house and knocked on the door. No one answered, meaning that she'd taken my advice and left Urbis completely. I opened the door, just to check, but her house was empty. It was much easier to get out of Urbis than it had been getting in. The whole of The Club District was deserted, and only a few stragglers were still exiting the doorway out of Cerce. I guided Elphin across the huge drawbridge with Lucy and Lepu still on his back and walked right into a sprawling mass of people. Tens of thousands of people had evacuated Urbis and were now standing around, each looking either scared or confused. I wanted to shout that the dragon was dead, but I couldn't be sure if that was the case. He'd completely disappeared, possibly hit by a Diamond Boulder. Instead, I wandered through the chaos, alternating between shouting Wisty and Vulpina. Lucy and Lepu joined in although we were pretty ineffectual in the melee and general noise of so many people.

"Rose!" I recognised Wisteria's voice after nearly an hour of searching. We found her right on the edge of the people in the Clublands.

"Lepu!" Vulpina launched herself at her brother and gave him a hug. "This is Wisty. She's awesome! She taught me some names of flowers and showed me which ones you could use to make a stew! She said we could come and visit her whenever we wanted!"

I smiled at Wisty. I knew Vulpina would come around within about three minutes in Wisty's company. She was a great nanny. It was highly unlikely that the royal Spade children would be allowed to run around in the Club District at any time in the future, however. The Spades, like the other suits, usually kept to their own districts.

"Wisty, I need to get these three home. The unicorn needs an animal doctor, too. Have you seen anyone around here that might be able to help us?"

Wisty looked past me through the throng of people. Then, with a shaky hand, she pointed out into the distance. At first, I didn't see what it was that she was pointing at. All I saw was a seething mass of people, mostly Clubs and Hearts. The Diamonds and Spades would have left their own districts from exits on the other side of Urbis, although I saw a scattering of both intermingled with the other people. It was only when I looked up that I saw what she was pointing at. On a hillside, right at the other side of the mass of people, was a dirigible. How had I forgotten? The hillside was the station for air travel in Vanatus and luckily for us, there was one ready to take off. I thanked Wisty and kissed her on her wrinkled cheek, before plonking all three children back on Elphin.

"Sorry, boy. Last time, I promise!"

I gave a last wave to Wisty, and we took off into the sky over the people towards the Dirigible.

"We're full!" replied a rather harassed acne-pocked youth, his Urbis Airlines cap sitting askew on his head and threatening to fall off completely. A throng of people were jockeying around him, desperate to get on. Honestly, one dragon sighting and everyone was fleeing the place. What happened to solidarity in times of hardship?

I pulled myself up to my full height (which was still a good seven inches shorter than the conductor who looked to be a Spade) and said the words I'd promised myself I'd never ever utter.

"Don't you know who I am?" Shame crept through me. I'd never once used my status to get what I wanted, but with three kidnapped royal children and an injured unicorn, I didn't feel that I had much choice)

"No, I don't know who you are," he replied tetchily. "Now, if you go to the back of the line, there will be another one here in a couple of hours".

So much for using my almighty fame to get what I wanted. The truth was, only the higher royals were really visible. Sage would have been able to get on here in a heartbeat. It shouldn't have surprised me that this man didn't know me, especially as he was not even a Club.

"Your highness!" I turned to see an old couple near the front of the line. Both had bowed their heads to me, but I could tell by their diminutive size and their pointed ears that they were Clubs.

"Your highness?" The conductor suddenly looked nervous, as though he'd not recognised someone of great importance, which of course he hadn't. Ha!

"This is her Royal highness, Princess Stargazer Lily of the Club Royal Family," the old man said to the conductor.

Wrong princess, but it made the conductor snap to attention.

"Your highness, forgive me, I didn't know".

I smiled at the old couple. Even though they had confused me with my sister, they had certainly got me the attention of the conductor, who was now opening the small door for me.

"It's not a problem." I let the children go ahead and then pulled Elphin toward the door.

"You can't take animals on there!" the conductor said, but a raised eyebrow from me had him backtracking. "Erm, I mean, it would be a pleasure to have your pet on board on this trip to Silverhaven."

Silverhaven was a distant city on the very far side of the Diamond Kingdom.

"I need to go to Mistdale!" Mistdale was the biggest city in The Clublands where the Club Royal family lived.

"The Mistdale Express is due in tonight. This one goes to Silverhaven."

I stood on my tiptoes, and when that didn't bring me eye to eye with him, I pulled on his tie until we were eye to eye.

"I need to get to Mistdale now!"

He pulled back, righted his hat and pulled the talk-piece for the tannoy to his mouth.

"This service will be now departing to Mistdale, I repeat, Mistdale only for this service."

A group of sorcerers, who were undoubtedly Diamonds, with their long robes stood to get off. All of them gave me filthy looks as they passed, but I didn't care. I wasn't here trying to make friends.

Because of the sudden change in destination, we had the whole place to ourselves, which was handy because it wasn't really built to take unicorns. The children and I sat at a table seat, whilst Elphin stood in the aisle. It turned out the conductor was going to journey with us.

"As we don't usually carry pets, I'm not sure how much to charge for him," he indicated Elphin, "but it's three hundred Denato for you and a hundred and fifty each for the children."

I was so glad we had already set off by this point, as I knew I didn't have a single Schillig to my name, let alone a Denato.

"I'm afraid I've left my money at home. I'll have someone send the appropriate funds to the Urbis Airlines head office as soon as I get back to the castle."

I could see his face drop as he realised he wasn't going to get a tip for his troubles. I suspect he'd lost a couple of juicy tips from the wealthy Diamonds, who had vacated the space because of us.

The journey was slow, and even though it can't have been any slower than my journey out on unicorn back, I didn't have the added excitement of chasing a dragon. The sun crept lower and lower in the sky until it dipped below the horizon. Had I really been away for so long? The children chatted amongst themselves, whilst I whiled away the hours by imagining my reception back at the castle. I would be a hero. No longer the lowliest of all the royal families, I'd be known as the brave one who saved the royal children by chasing a dragon across the country. Even the Queen of Hearts would have to bow down to me after saving her youngest daughter. The thought made me smile. It was actually a pleasant ride back, imagining the Queen of Hearts grovelling at my feet.

The Clublands below us were dark in the night sky, but there were the occasional collections of lights where small villages were. Eventually, I saw the bright lights of Mistdale up ahead. The lights were much more concentrated here as Mistdale was the capital of The Clublands, but it was still nothing compared to the huge urban sprawl of Urbis. The dirigible landed at the designated station, which was a couple of miles from the castle. I wasn't sure how we were going to make that particular journey, as I was reluctant to put any more pressure on poor Elphin, and the three kids had fallen asleep. I didn't fancy carrying them across town. If I was lucky, I might be able to hire a Shire horse, which was the way the people of Mistdale got around. As it turned out, getting to the castle was not going to be a problem. A huge throng of people had gathered at the station to greet us. I wondered how they all knew we were even on the dirigible.

I shook the children awake. Lucy and Vulpina opened their eyes wearily, but Lepu remained fast asleep. I picked him up, ushered the two girls out in front of me, and guided Elphin out of the small door. The riotous applause from the people took me by surprise. Reporters from The Club Gazette jostled for position amongst the reporters from the other newspapers. Flashes of light blinded me and told me that the reporters had brought photographers with them.

I gave an uneasy smile and waved at the people, all the while trying to remember my princess training and the correct etiquette.

A huge squeal cut through the throng, and the Queen of Hearts came running up to us. She picked Lucy up and hugged her tight. Barely a second later, the Queen of Spades followed suit with her own children. After hugging Vulpina, she carefully took her sleeping son from my arms. Neither woman spoke to me, but The Queen of Diamonds gave me a grateful smile as she took her daughter's hand and disappeared back into the crowd.

I was suddenly alone in a sea of people. Microphones were thrust into my face, and I still couldn't see with all the flashes. Someone, I couldn't see who, grabbed my arm and threw me into a carriage. As the only people who used carriages were the Royals, dignitaries, and merchants, I guessed it was one of my family who had grabbed me. When my eyes finally cleared, I was surprised to see Tree sitting opposite me.

"Tree!"

"Ma'am, your parents asked me to collect you and bring you back to the castle."

"Ok," something was going on. The way he spoke, with reservation, made me think that something had happened in my absence. "Has something happened, Tree?"

"Happened, ma'am?"

"I was just wondering why my parents didn't come to collect me themselves."

"No reason, ma'am." He was lying, but I didn't want to press him.

"There is an injured unicorn back at the station. We need to go back and get him!" I couldn't believe I'd forgotten Elphin.

"The castle vets have already been dispatched to collect the animal."

"Oh!" I said for want of anything else to say.

Feeling vastly underwhelmed by my reception now that the braying packs of reporters were behind us, I felt as though the last twelve hours had all been a dream. A yawn escaped me, and I became aware of just how tired I actually was. Now that the adrenaline had subsided, I felt more exhausted than I had ever felt in my life. I closed my eyes, and it was only when I was on the very edge of oblivion that I realised that I'd left my sword in the Heart district.

I woke up to the sound of people arguing. Tree held my hand as I exited the carriage. Sorrell was there to greet me. She came up to me and gave me a hug.

"Thank goodness, you are safe."

"Who is that arguing?" I asked. "It was too distant to make out what was being argued about, but there were a lot of angry people shouting at each other. With a start, I recognised one as my father.

"It doesn't matter right now. Are you injured at all?" She looked down at my singed dress.

"I don't think so." The truth was, I'd been running on pure adrenaline all day, and I'd not even taken time out to assess if I was damaged at all. My whole body felt heavy with fatigue, but nothing hurt unduly.

"Nevertheless, the court physician has been instructed to see you in your room."

"What's happening, Sorrell?" Something really was off, and it was beginning to make me feel nervous. I'd saved royal Children from a dragon, hadn't I? I'd expected a bit more of a welcome home than being ushered into my room quietly by my sister.

Sorrell pecked me on the cheek and left me to go into my room alone, leaving my question unanswered. The castle doctor was a large friendly woman who by coincidence was actually named Doc, short for Dockleaf. As I was rarely ill, I almost never had cause to see her, but I knew her well from various childhood illnesses. She'd sat by my bedside for three weeks when I had dragon fever at six years old.

"Hi, Doc!" I said wearily. I wanted nothing more than to curl up in bed and sleep for a week.

"What have yer been gettin' yerself into now then, Honey?" She spoke with a Redfall Accent. Redfall was a small agricultural town on the edge of Clubland, well known for two things, beautiful beaches and fertile soil. That was where we got most of our vegetables from.

"I killed a Dragon."

"Did yer now?" She seemed completely unfazed by my proclamation. "Let's be seeing you then."

I let Doc peel my clothing from me. The charred remains of the dress fell to the floor along with the armour until I was stood there in just my underwear.

My arms and my legs below the knee were filthy, and the stench of smoke was unmistakable.

"What a mess yer are now. You've got a bit of a burn on your arm but nothing that a bit of my magic burn cream won't cure. You should be bathing before I apply it, though. You'll not be wanting to wash it off."

I looked down at my arm. I'd not even noticed I had been burned at all, but the skin looked red and had blistered in a couple of places. I guess I'd gotten off lightly.

"I've already run a bath for you, chicken."

I entered the little bathroom that ran off from my bedroom and gratefully sank into the hot water. As it was Club water. It had soothing properties of its own. I could almost feel the heat of my burn leave me, even though the bath water was piping hot. Club water was not only the only magic Clubs possessed, it was also our biggest commodity. All the other suits wanted it, the Hearts, especially, as they used it in all their face creams and potions. Because of that, we were able to sell it at a premium, which irked the Hearts no end. They thought that because it was water and it was natural, they should be entitled to it for free. The problem with that was, the magic spring was on Clubland soil, way up in the Dragon Mountains, and the stream meandered through our kingdom until it reached the ocean. At no point did it flow through Heart land, so they had to pay. As they made plenty of money back on all the potions they used it for, I didn't think they had any reason to complain. Quite a few of my sisters bought makeup and skin creams from the Heart District of Urbis. The Hearts did all right by us.

I washed my hair using a strongly scented shampoo to get rid of the sooty smell and got out of the bath, dripping water all over the stone floor in the process. Wrapping a clean towel around myself, I entered my bedroom once again.

"There yer are, all nice and clean. Let me look at yer arm now I can see it all proper like".

I held out my arm, The redness had all but gone, leaving just a couple of blisters.

"Almost as good as new, eh?" said Doc, scrabbling around in her doctor's bag. I'm not even sure yer'll need some of my magic cream on yer, but I'll put just a bit on for safe measure."

I held out my arm for the 'magic' cream, too exhausted to argue. The cream was not magic. It was nothing more than a normal burn cream, but Doc liked to call it such as she had done with every medicine she'd ever given me from cough syrup to dragon drops.

"Yer'll be needin' yer rest now, Lovie," she packed her cream into the large leather bag and made for the door. "Tomorrow, yer arm will be right as rain."

I smiled at her and then fell into bed, where I fell asleep almost straight away.

January 2nd

The sound of knocking woke me from my slumber. Light poured through my window meaning it was pretty late. Being the middle of winter, the sun didn't rise until about ten o'clock. I pulled on a robe and opened the door. The corridor was empty in both directions, but copies of the Club Gazette, Heart Echo, and Spade Chronicle had been left outside my door. Someone would have had to go to a lot of trouble to get the latter two. They were only published in their own Kingdoms, and when we did get them, they were usually a day out of date. They were only sold in The Clublands for the tourists and seeing as there weren't many tourists in The Clublands, getting them was pretty rare. What was even rarer was getting a copy with today's date. The only one missing was the Diamond Times. As the furthest Kingdom from The Clublands, I suspected it would turn up later. I picked up the papers and took them back to bed. As getting papers was such a rarity, I expected that there must be something about me in them, else why would they have been left for me? I pulled the Heart Echo towards me and unfolded it. Nothing could have prepared me for what I was about to see. Not the smiling face of myself getting off the dirigible, looking heroic with three rescued children I'd expected but a photo of me in Cerce with the word 'Murderer' emblazoned across the front.

"What the?" I unfolded the other two papers. They had the same picture but vastly differing headlines. The Gazette read "Royal Rescue Ruination." The Chronicle's headline was even more disturbing. 'Royal Club Unearths Spade Secret. Queen goes into hiding.'

I couldn't understand what I was reading. I studied the photo again. It was of me holding the man in the alley in Cerce, just as he died. Where had this come from? I'd been alone in that alley. And then I remembered the flashes. I'd assumed it was lightning and with everything going on, had failed to notice that no thunder had accompanied it. There must have been a photographer in one of the buildings taking photos from the window. Why hadn't he helped? He must have been able to see that I was struggling.

Putting my annoyance with the photographer to one side, I brought my attention back to the Heart Newspaper.

Murderer? Who was I supposed to have murdered? The man had had Dragon Fire breathed all over him. I'd tried to save him.

I tried to ignore the huge picture of me taking up the front page and instead moved my eyes down to the article in The Echo.

Disbelief flooded through the people of Cerce yesterday as a Club Royal Princess, known as Rose, the number two of the royal family, chased a dragon into our district. The dragon then went on to rampage through the town, demolishing both residential and commercial buildings including the famous Alchemy Bar on Griffin Street. Our reporter then observed further destruction at the hands of The Diamonds who waged war on The Heart District by sending magical boulders crashing down demolishing even more of our district. In a bizarre turn of events, the young royal, who herself professes to be a warrior, flamed the dragon using a flame gun, which she stole from a shop. The dragon turned out to be a Spade dragon shifter by the name of Drage Fortis. This same Spade, who was an aid to the Spade Royal Family, confessed just before dying that two of the youngest royal Spade children were actually his, borne of an illegitimate affair with The Queen of Spades. The Queen has since taken her youngest offspring and gone into hiding. Whether Rose Club will be tried for the murder of Fortis remains to be seen.

I threw the paper to one side in shock. Murderer! It was right there in black and white. I'd killed someone. I had no defence for my actions. How could I have known that the Dragon was a Spade? I tried to think back about whether I might have seen some sign that the dragon was part human, but I'd been so caught up in trying to save the children that it just hadn't occurred to me to check. There were subtle differences between shifters and true animals. Just as when the shifters were in human form, they held some of their animal characteristics, the same held true for them in animal form. The man I'd killed for example. If I'd thought about it, the flaming red hair should have been a bit of a giveaway. How would I have known that he was half-human when he was in his dragon form though? It's certainly trickier but not impossible. The shifter animals have a human gait to them. From what I know about shifters, they think as humans even in their animal form although they also possess their animal senses. Generally, they are better than most humans in almost every way. As a dragon, Drage would have been thinking like a human, so why didn't he stop?

"No!" I said aloud. I couldn't have known. He was behaving exactly like a Dragon. There was nothing human in his actions. No one could have known. Could they?

I didn't want to read the other papers. I was a murderer and nothing they said could change that. Warriors don't cry, and I didn't want to, but tears pricked at the corners of my eyes. Someone knocked at my door, and I quickly wiped the moisture away with the back of my sleeve.

"Rose?"

It was Sage. He was the favourite of all my brothers, but it was extremely rare he came to see me in my room. He was usually so busy tending to his important royal duties. Then I realised that having a member of the royal family murder someone from another suit would probably count as important. I felt sorry for him, knowing the mess this would cause. The Club standing in the world would suffer greatly from this.

"Hey," His voice was soothing and not in the least bit angry. It was something to be grateful for at least.

"Rose," he pulled me towards him and held me tight, stroking my hair. Looking after his little sister wasn't part of his job description, but I was so glad he was doing it. I don't think I'd have coped if my mother or father had come in. My mother would have fretted and made me feel even worse, whilst my father would have lectured me for making a mockery of Club Royalty.

All Sage did was stroke my hair until the sobs subsided. I'd never been more grateful that he was my brother.

"What's going to happen to me, Sage?" I asked when I was finally able to get a word out. I waited, knowing that a jail sentence was the likely option, although the death sentence wouldn't be completely out of the question. It depended on just how high this went. I killed a Spade, but I did it in the Heart district. I had no idea whose jurisdiction that would fall under.

"For the time being, nothing. I'm not going to pretend that this isn't a complete mess, but Father is in talks to try and sort through the issues. The Hearts are calling for the death sentence..."

"Shit!"

"...But, Father won't allow it. He's called an emergency meeting with the Aces, and there has been a block put in place to prevent you from being removed from The Clublands. You do have to remain in the castle for the time being, but I'm pretty sure that won't be a problem for you."

"But what's going to happen? The Queen of Spades..."

Sage interrupted me.

"Everything is up in the air at the moment. This is a completely unprecedented situation, and no one knows what's going to happen. It goes without saying that the other suits have left the castle. I think we just need to leave it up to those people above us."

I smiled. Sage was about as high as you could get. I'd completely thrown him into the shit.

"I murdered a man," I said in a small voice. I was aware how pathetic I sounded. I'd usually hate showing weakness, but at that moment, I wanted nothing more than to feel comforted. For someone to tell me that this would all go away, that it was all a horrible nightmare that I would wake up from any second.

"Look at me." He tipped my chin upwards, so I was looking into his eyes. "Without you, who knows what would have happened to those children. There was no way you could have known he was a Spade. If it were up to me, they would be ordering you a medal right now. There aren't many people who would fight a dragon."

"Yeah, no one is as stupid as I am." Oh Monsatsu, here came the one-person pity party.

"Brave is the word I would have used."

I loved how he was doing his best to make me feel better, but whatever way he phrased it, it didn't change the fact that I had killed a man.

"Did Drage have children?" The thought that he had a wife and family back home was almost too much to bear.

"Apart from the two by the Queen of Spades, you mean? No, I don't think so. As far as I've been able to tell, he was a courtier in the palace. Whether or not he really did father her two children is unknown at this point, although the Queen going into hiding is rather suspicious. It makes it look as though she was guilty of having an affair. The problem with Spades is, it's not like they get their colouring from their parents. They are a strange breed. If a Club with black hair has children with another club with black hair, their offspring will also have black hair and will take on other characteristics of each parent. The same goes for the Hearts and the Diamonds. The Spades on the other hand, well you've seen it yourself. The King is a dog, The Queen, a cat, and they have all manner of offspring, none of which look the same or shift into the same animal. It's a strange magic. The father could be anyone. The King has asked that one of the Diamonds come to his palace to perform some kind of magical test to determine the children's parentage, but he's going to have trouble doing that unless they find the Queen and her children."

"A wolf and a leopard."

"What?"

"The King and Queen of Spades, they are not a dog and a cat; they are a wolf and a leopard." Normally, I would have felt better that I was not the only one who had made the wrong distinction. Today, though, I didn't give a rat's ass what the King and Queen of Spade's shifter form was.

"Really? Hmmm. You learn something new every day." He raised an eyebrow thoughtfully.

"So what now, Sage?"

"Now, you just stay here whilst father and his council figure out what to do. I'm going to go and join them so I'll be able to keep you updated. I don't want you to worry, though, Squirt. There is no way Father will let anything happen to you. Anyone with half a brain can see that you saved those children's lives. We'll have this whole thing sorted out before you know it."

I wish I could have been so sure. His words, although well-meaning, did nothing to truly comfort me. He gave me one last stroke on the head and left me alone with my thoughts.

I'd barely had time to compose myself when there was another knock on the door. Star opened it and came in without waiting for me to say 'enter.'

"Oh Rose!" she flung herself on me and burst into tears. I would have joined her, but she was shedding enough tears for both of us. Star was known for being the most emotional one of the family, and it was I that ended up comforting her, which strangely helped me to feel better too. Just knowing that my family were on my side made all the difference

"Did you read the papers?" she managed between hiccups. "I thought you should know what was going on before anyone came to see you. None of us were allowed to come to you before Sage told you exactly what had happened, but I thought you'd want to know the truth."

"Thanks, Star. Sage didn't seem to know much more than what was in the papers. He told me that the Hearts want my head on a plate, but Father wouldn't let them take me."

"Of course, he wouldn't. You did nothing wrong."

"I killed a person, Star." She winced as I said it. It took everything I had not to do the same myself.

"You know that I'm an animal lover and in any other circumstance would hate the killing of a dragon or any other creature, but you had to save those children. What else could you have done?"

That was huge coming from Star, who cared about dragons and other animals much more than she cared about people. There was not much use pointing out that the dragon was actually a person. It wouldn't have made the killing of him any worse in her eyes. She viewed all living creatures as equals.

"Sage said the same thing."

"Of course, he did." She sat silently for a moment, looking like she was contemplating telling me something. I hoped it wasn't something that would make my situation worse. Although, for the life of me, I couldn't think of a single thing that could make it worse.

"The Hearts have sent some of their best warriors up into the mountains to kill the dragons up there."

I could tell, just by looking at her that the thought of dragons being killed for something that wasn't their fault was beyond her comprehension. The tears in her eyes began to fall again, smudging the intricate floral design she'd painted on herself today.

So the Hearts were taking this out on the dragons? I wondered why. They knew that the dragon that destroyed part of their city wasn't part of the dragon colony from the Dragon Mountains. Their own paper had said as much. I suspected that there was an ulterior motive, but what?

"They can't do anything to the dragons. They are protected by law," I said to placate her. Some laws differed between kingdoms, but the law regarding magical creatures, among others, was laid down in Urbis by the Aces. The King and Queen would be insane to go against Urbis law. Mind you, sanity was not a strong point of the Queen of Hearts.

"That's just it. They don't care. They say that if you are allowed to kill dragons, then they should be able to, too. They are just using it as an excuse to get their skin to make dragon-hide bags and shoes."

"But that's stupid! I killed that dragon because I had to, and he wasn't even a dragon."

"They don't care. It's just an excuse." She wiped her damp cheek and the flowers were obliterated, leaving an inky green and pink smear on her cheek.

"They have to cross into Club territory to get up to the mountains. Father will never let them."

"They've already gone."

"What do the Spades and Diamonds think of this?" I asked, genuinely curious.

"The Spade King is so angry at the moment anyway, probably because his wife was having an affair, and he's become somewhat of a laughing stock. He seems to have taken a dislike of dragons. The Diamonds have kept a low profile on the matter so far. I think they want to retend that they weren't involved even though a lot of this mess is down to them plundering in with their trebuchet and magic boulders."

I suddenly felt even worse. I'd caused such a mess; I didn't even know where to begin to resolve it. Not that I could anyway, confined to the castle as I was.

"I'm sorry, Star."

"Oh, no, please don't be sorry. I'm not blaming you. I just thought you should know what's going on."

"So let me get this straight. The Spade Queen had an affair with one of her courtiers and had two children. The guy she had the children by was Drage, a dragon shifter. For whatever reason, he finally flipped and decided to kidnap his children back, accidentally taking a Heart child with him. I chase him, not realising he is a shifter and kill him, although not before he's rampaged all through Urbis. I bring the children back. The Spade Queen immediately takes her children and goes into hiding. The Spades now hate Dragons, and their kingdom is in disarray because their Queen is gone, and their King is furious. The Hearts hate Dragons, me, and Diamonds because between us we demolished Cerce and kidnapped their youngest royal,"

"And have very expensive skin that can be made into bags," interrupted Star.

"That, too. We are in a mess because it all happened whilst everyone was here and both the Spades and Hearts hate us because our security wasn't enough to stop Dragons coming into the castle and kidnapping children. The Hearts want me to be executed for murder, although the Spade King would probably congratulate me for killing his wife's paramour. And father can't stop the Hearts coming into our land to get to the mountains to kill the dragons, who are, in fact, the only innocent ones in all this."

"Yep, that pretty much sums it all up," said Star glumly. "There is one good thing about all of this, though."

"Really?" I couldn't see a single good thing at all.

"The Spades didn't want the unicorn back. It belonged to the Queen. The King said we could keep him. I don't think he could bear to look at anything that the Queen owned and, well, as the Queen has disappeared, I've been allowed to keep him."

Being able to keep Elphin was a huge deal for Star. Magical creatures were extremely rare and, as such, were very valuable. Even though, as royals, we were the richest people in the Club Kingdom, we still lagged far behind in regards to riches compared to the other ruling families of Vanatus. A Unicorn was way beyond what we'd be able to afford.

"His name is Elphin. How is he?" Another innocent victim in all this. Honestly, I don't know how I could feel any worse.

"He's fine. I've made up some burn cream, which is working a treat. Once his scorched hair grows out, he'll be almost as good as new. His wingtip will always be short of a few feathers but that shouldn't harm his ability to fly."

"That's great news, Star!" She could add him to her menagerie of animals. If there was ever an injured animal to care for, Star would be there. She didn't have pets, as such; she had a whole zoo of creatures. Elphin would be the pride of her collection.

"I should probably go. I had to beg to come and see you as it was. I think Mother and Father will be up to see you as soon as they know what's going on."

"Thanks for coming up, Star, and thanks for the papers." I hugged her again. I was lucky to have such great brothers and sisters.

"Everything will be ok."

When she left, I thought about her last words to me. The exact same sentiment Sage had said before he had left. I wondered if they both really knew I'd be ok or if they were just empty words said to buoy me up, make me feel better. It was more than likely the latter. Everything was such a mess, and at the end of the day, if both the Hearts wanted me executed, even the Aces would have to bow down to the pressure.

I read the other two papers. Same story, different spin. The Club Gazette painted me as a wronged hero who had bravely gone into battle with a kidnapper; whereas, the Chronicle made sensationalist claims about their Queen, and I was just a side story of no importance. It was amazing how one story could be told with so many different angles. I wondered how The Diamond Times would paint this. Apart from the fact that the Hearts now hated them, and the Hearts seemed to hate everyone; the Diamonds had got out of this whole debacle relatively unscathed. It would be interesting to see how they painted the picture and whose side they would take. On one hand, they got all of their fine clothes from the Hearts, but they got the water that they used in the mines from us. There was something about the water's magical properties that made the diamonds sparkle within the ore, making them more easily spotted. Of course, the Spades worked in the mines so it wouldn't do the Diamonds any good to take sides at all.

The day dragged on with no more visitors, save for a kitchen maid bringing me food. As it was leftover Toadspawn stew, I put it to one side. Even the most succulent dish wouldn't have appealed to me, though. My stomach churned which had nothing to do with lack of food. Every time I heard a noise, my stomach leapt, wondering if it was either of my parents coming to tell me that the death penalty had been ordered.

It was nearly seven o'clock at night before Tree came to get me.

"Your mother requests your presence in her chambers."

"Since when have you ever spoken to me so formally? And since when has mother not just come to see me when she wants to?" I knew I was sounding more snarky than I had any right to be and it wasn't Tree's fault, but I'd been left alone all day, not knowing whether I'd live or die."

"I'm sorry, Rose. The Queen has wanted to come and see you all day, but she has been busy with dealing with all the problems. You've seen the papers, and so have the people. They are getting anxious, and a lot of them have been congregating outside the palace demanding answers."

"Answers about what?" I was genuinely confused. This might have been a mess, but I didn't see how it would impact on our subjects.

"They are scared. They think there might be a war."

"War?" It hadn't occurred to me how far-reaching this could be I suddenly felt very ashamed about being annoyed that no one had been to visit me.

"There are Heart soldiers all over the Clubland. The Spade Kingdom is up in arms, and no one knows what's going on. The Queen has spent the day trying to appease them. Your father is in talks with his council and leaders of all the other suits. He has been summoned to Urbis to speak with The Aces, which is why he hasn't been to see you. Everyone is running scared at the moment, and no one knows what to do."

"Oh," I said. What else was there to say? Only I could do something so catastrophic that would result in a war of all the suits in her first year of being a full royal.

My mother had her back to me as I entered the room. Either she didn't hear the door open or didn't want to face me, but I had to call her name to get her to turn round. Tree closed the door behind me, leaving us alone.

"Rose." My mother had tears streaming down her face and somehow her beauty had faded overnight. I wanted more than anything to run to her and sit in her lap and have her sing to me as she did when I was a child. Instead, she just stood there silently looking at me as if she didn't quite know what to say. I'd rarely ever seen her cry before, but she seemed to be doing nothing but in the last few days.

"I'm sorry, Mama." I hung my head in shame. The thought that I'd hurt this amazing woman was almost too much to bear.

"No!"

She spoke so sharply that I looked up, wondering if there was someone else in the room to whom she was speaking.

"Don't you say you are sorry to me, Rose." Her voice still had a hard edge, but her eyes were full of nothing but love. "In all my life, I have never met anyone as brave as you showed yourself to be yesterday. You've spent a lifetime telling me how much you detested being a princess and how much you wanted to be a warrior; and I, for my part, played it down, told you that you couldn't. I denied you the one thing that you wanted above all else. Yesterday, you showed me the warrior that you really are. It is I who should be sorry, Rose."

I just stood there, not knowing what to say. For as long as I could remember, she had made me wear pretty dresses and taught me how to be a lady, and now, here she was, telling me I was a warrior.

"When this mess is sorted out, I'm letting you join your elder brothers in training to be a warrior. You are as brave as they are, if not more so. The courage you showed yesterday..." she trailed off.

I could barely believe what I was hearing.

"Are you sure?"

"The way things are going, it looks like we are going to need all the warriors we can get." She said it as a half-hearted joke, but like all the best jokes, it was based on truth.

I ran over to her and threw my arms around her. I could feel the dampness on her cheeks. To be a warrior was my dream, not the one she had for me. I was comforting her and not the other way round.

"What about..." I didn't have to say it. She knew what I was about to say.

"You did what you had to do. If you hadn't killed that man, the children would probably have perished. The Diamonds were attacking him. If they had scored a direct hit, the children would have been killed. Don't for a second think that you are anything but a hero. All this would have happened with or without you chasing that dragon. The only difference is, you managed to get three innocent children home."

"But if I hadn't chased him, at least then, the Hearts and the Spades wouldn't hate us so much."

My mother gave a mirthless laugh.

"The Queen of Hearts blamed us for the dragon right from the start. It was our fault, you see, lack of security. It had nothing to do with the fact that the nanny let the children stand by the open window. You should have heard her. When we heard that you had rescued the children, I actually heard her say that she thought you were the only Club with backbone. She said it under her breath, of course, but I heard. You showed her what Clubs are made of!"

"She really said that? About me?" I was amazed. The woman hated my guts.

"She did, indeed. You showed true grit out there yesterday, and as soon as your Father sorts this all out, you'll be free to do what you please. Unfortunately, until then, we have to abide by the law, and you have to stay within the grounds." She pulled away from me and fetched a box from the side of the room.

"This is for you. Sage told me that you might need it in warrior school."

I opened the box to find a green tunic embroidered with pink roses. Star must have been busy these past few hours. I'd recognise her work anywhere. There were also some green leggings, a pair of brown leather shoes, and a brown leather belt with a silver buckle. It had the Club Army Emblem on it. Three circles joined in a triangle with a triangle at the bottom.

Even though Star had gone to a lot of trouble making me the clothes, it was something else, laid on top that made my heart beat faster with excitement.

Laid out on top, ready for battle was a large sword. It was brand new, so unlike the old second-hand sword I'd been using for practice, the one I'd lost in the Heart District. This one shone. It was so bright and polished that I could see the look of wonder on my own face reflected in it.

"Thank you!"

"You earned it, Rose."

I held up the sword. It was a lot heavier than I was used to. Out of the corner of my eye, I could see my mother watching me.

"Do you really think there is going to be a war?" I put the sword back in the box, both eager to practice with it and scared at what it represented.

"It looks that way. I truly hope I'm wrong and this all blows over, but the people are scared, people of all suits. It's not just about the Queen of Diamonds or the Queen of Hearts; it goes much deeper. What happened yesterday was just a catalyst. There are rebellions going on between lots of people and to be honest, I don't know exactly what is happening myself. The King is in crisis talks. He's been trying to sort it out all day, but with the media saying one thing and the people saying another, it's difficult to unravel exactly what's going on. It's much more complicated than what happened yesterday. Years of simmering bitterness between suits and between people within their own suits. Quite frankly, it's a bit of a mess, but your father knows what he is doing, and I have trust that he will lead us in the right direction. Until then, you need to have lessons with that sword, and if I'm right, there is a lesson first thing tomorrow morning. I've told Wulfric to expect you."

I hugged my mother one more time, and she gave me a sad smile.

"I had to pull an awful lot of strings to get this place for you, so make sure you turn up on time. Only the elder royal sons and the best of the very best of our subjects are allowed to train with Wulfric. So there will be a lot of angry people down there, Rose. They are going to be out to prove that you don't belong. I want you to show them. I saw what you did yesterday, and I have complete faith in you. Others might not see it that way. Watch your back."

I could barely believe how the day had turned out. I'd woken up feeling like a hero, only to read the papers and find out I was a murderer and had ignited what looked like a war between the suits. Then my own mother, who had spent my entire childhood telling me to be more ladylike, was now telling me to go out and learn to fight for our country.

I felt better than I had all day. Looking at it logically, The Diamonds would probably have hit Drage anyway if I'd not been there. Even if he'd escaped, there would have been an angry mob after him, and if there was one thing I knew about angry mobs, it was that they shoot first and ask questions later. I briefly wondered where Drage was heading with the children and if he had a plan or if he was just flying wildly with them. I guessed no one would ever know, at least, not until the Queen of Spades turned up again, if she ever did.

I went back to my room and waited for someone to call me to take me to see my father. By the time it got to ten o'clock, I realised he wasn't going to come. Whatever decision was going to be made about my future had not yet been decided. Sleep was almost an impossible feat. Dreams of dragons and lynch mobs interspersed with thoughts of finally realising my dream, making the night a bumpy one. When the next day dawned, I was up and ready for what lay ahead

January 3rd

After changing into my new training outfit, I meandered slowly through the castle corridors, just waiting for someone to grab me and force me to go back into my room. Despite what my mother had said about being free to move about the castle and grounds, I was still a murderer, and the death sentence still loomed above my head. The corridors were strangely quiet. Usually a hive of activity, now they were deserted, and I didn't see a single member of my family or one of the staff until I got to the large log wall of the training ground. I looked up at the gates, the same ones I'd watched my brothers go through daily and wished I was with them. Today I would be.

Despite my early start, I was the last to enter the large training grounds. The log wall ran around a sandy arena lit by hundreds of flaming torches driven into the ground. I tried to overlook the obvious fire hazard and, instead, turned my attention onto the equipment that had been set out, ready for use. On the far side were hanging effigies made out of sand bags with targets painted in the centre. Huge circular targets stood at the left-hand side, obviously for archery practice. The rest of the arena was empty, although various white lines were painted on the ground. At least a hundred young men stood around waiting for Wulfric, the Head of the Training Academy. I'd only met him once, a hugely muscled man with tattoos covering both his arms and a large grey handlebar moustache obscuring most of the lower part of his face. It made up for the fact that the rest of his head was bald.

Some of the boys were fighting with each other, mock battles or wrestling practice. One group were examining a number of weapons, and others stood around talking. I recognised none of them, but they all had one thing in common. They were all huge. The Clubs were a very short race so to see so many tall people in one place was quite a shock. There was not a single one that didn't tower over me by at least a foot. I looked around desperately. I knew Sage wouldn't be here. He was too busy dealing with the same stuff as my father, but my other brothers would be. My second eldest brother would fit in with these other boys and would be hard to spot, but the others had the same stature as me and would stick out like sore thumbs. Sequoia was the tallest in our family but even he'd be dwarfed next to these guys.

Before I had the chance to find any of my brothers, a huge hairy hand rested itself on my shoulder, almost knocking me to the ground. I turned to find Wulfric standing right behind me. My eyes were roughly at the same height as the buckle on his belt. There was no way he was a full Club. He must have inherited a little Diamond in his ancestry at some point. Diamonds were the tallest race in Vanatus, most of them stood over six feet tall.

"So, you want to be a warrior?" His voice boomed out across the training ground, and, immediately, all the boys stopped what they were doing and turned towards us. They organised themselves, like little ants, into perfectly straight rows, each one saluting Wulfric by holding their right hand in the air with the three middle fingers raised, which was the standard Club salute. Now that the boys stood side by side, I could see my brothers. Sequoia was in the front row with an empty space next to him. It must have been for the one absent warrior in training, Sage.

I felt so intimidated with these huge boys staring me that I forgot to answer Wulfric. His grip tightened on my shoulder.

"Let me tell you something Princess. I don't let just anyone into my army. Just because you are a princess, don't expect any favours from me. If you don't live up to my expectations, you'll be out, do you understand?"

I was under no illusion that his expectations of me were incredibly low. For that reason alone, my fears fell away. I might not be anywhere near as big or strong as these men, but I wasn't the pathetic little girl he'd pegged me to be.

"I can do this!"

Wulfric dropped his hand and stared at me. He'd obviously not expected me to reply to him. I don't think he was used to people answering him back.

"You can, can you?" He eyed me with almost contempt in his expression. "What's your skill, Princess? Sword fighting, eh?" He brought his attention to the sword at my side.

"Oaken!" He shouted to one of the boys in the line. He was the largest of them all and built like an Oak Tree. His muscles rippled under his tunic, which was ever so slightly too tight whether by design or inability to afford a newer one, I didn't know. He was also extremely attractive. Shit! The last thing I needed was to be pitted against a pretty boy.

"Sir!"

"Come here. I want you to show the princess here what you can do."

The hulking giant walked forward, bridging the gap between us and the rest of the boys. About half way across the arena, he stopped and began to swipe his sword around. It cut through the air, as he swung it around over his head in a figure eight pattern, all the while grunting in, what was meant to be an intimidating manner but sounded a little like a wild boar.

He was actually pretty impressive. The sword moved so quickly that it was almost impossible to see. His swordmanship was almost dancelike and I began to rethink my first impression of him. I could learn a thing or two from his deft swordwork. I tried to follow his moves with my eyes but then he grunted once more and lowered his sword to his side.

"This is what we do here, Princess," said Wulfric. "Do you want to go back to mummy yet?"

Something snapped in me. Who did he think he was? Hadn't he heard that I'd killed a dragon only yesterday? Yeah, this Oaken dude might be pretty nifty but I was hardly a toddler with a wooden knife.

I felt my grip on the sword tighten and before I had a chance to think reasonably I raised it above my head and charged at Oaken. To give him his due, he responded quickly to my attack and blocked me before I brought the sword right down on his head. I'd not wanted to injure him. I knew he'd block me, but I was glad to see the look of shock in his eyes. I pulled back and almost danced around him as I thrust my sword one more time. He raised his sword to block, but I was already around on his other side. This continued for a good few minutes, me thrusting my sword, him trying to block, only to find me not there anymore. At any point, I could have stuck the sword right in his gut, but I didn't. He might have been huge and skilled, but I was fast and in this game, speed beat strength every time. His huge size was to my advantage as I had more places to stick my sword. Oaken, on the other hand, was having great difficulty even seeing me. I was small and didn't stay still long enough to be hit. Just like the dragon, he was an easy target purely because he was so large. I grinned at him and arched my brow, mocking him. He didn't take it well and instead of playing fair, lunged towards me. I wasn't ready for his change in tactics and fell backwards onto the sandy ground, his full weight on top of me, knocking the wind out of me. I found myself looking up into cerulean eyes, a rarity among Clubs. We usually had eye colours ranging from bog brown to mush green.

"Not so clever now are you, Princess?" He said echoing Wulfric's derogatory term. I could feel his warm breath on me, and despite my anger at the way he was talking to me, something stirred within me. I could barely breath because of the weight of his body crushing me. I could feel the rippled muscles on his torso pushing down. It hurt but it felt good too. Then I became aware of something else. When I looked down our bodies, I saw my sword raised upwards. It had cut right through the fabric of his tunic between his body and his arm. A millimetre to the right or left and I'd have nicked his skin. I'd won the fight, and when I looked into his eyes I could see that he knew it. With all the strength I could muster, I pushed him off of me and pulled myself out from under him, dusting my clothes off as I stood.

"And don't call me Princess," I said out loud. "My name is Rose!"

The arena was silent. A hundred men looked at me with a mixture of awe and shock on their faces. Someone in the crowd clapped, followed by another then another. Sequoia smiled at me, and I saw an almost imperceptible nod of the head. I grinned as the clapping thundered around the stadium.

"Enough!" A voice yelled above the noise, and the men became silent.

"Very nice, Rose." I turned to see Wulfric moving towards me. I might have been wrong but, just for a second, I noticed a hint of admiration in his eyes. He turned to the rest of the men. "Right, on with training. I've had an order from the King; we need to gear up for battle. Oaken, get up. You can partner with Rose here. If you are lucky, maybe she will teach you a few things, huh?"

"Yessir!" Oaken stood, a gaping hole down the right-hand side of his tunic. He saluted Wulfric and grimaced at me. I guess I had made another enemy. I mentally added him to the list of people I'd annoyed or upset in the last twenty-four hours. It was shaping up to be quite a list.

As the men drifted to different parts of the arena, Wulfric lowered himself to my height and spoke in my ear. For once, the message was only for me.

"You impressed me back there, but don't think that means you get a free pass. You got lucky. I'll be keeping an eye on you, do you understand me?"

"Yes sir." I saluted him. Despite his warnings and harsh words, I knew I had what it took, and he knew it, too. I smiled to myself as I walked towards my new partner. Oaken wouldn't know what was coming.

***

"Get off me, you brute!" I tried to squirm out from under Oaken's grip, but I literally could not move a millimetre. His weight crushed me, rendering me barely able to breathe. This time it wasn't nice. He was pushing himself down as if to prove he could beat me. When he saw that he had won, he stood, releasing me from the crushing weight. He held out his hand to help me up, which I completely ignored, getting up from the rough ground myself. I could see Wulfric chuckling in the background.

"That wasn't fair," I yelled.

"We are training for war," replied Oaken grinning, "not going to a party. War isn't fair. Do you think that your enemy will play fair with you?"

"I could have beaten you in a second if you let me use my sword," I replied, doubled over, trying to get my breath back.

"I don't doubt it, but Wulfric asked me to teach you hand-to-hand combat, so that's what I'm doing."

"But you are so much bigger than me," I whined. If I wasn't careful, he'd go back to calling me Princess, and then if Wulfric caught on, I'd be out. Why did we have to start with hand-to-hand combat? Oaken was so much stronger than I, I couldn't hope to beat him. If they'd let me start on archery or knife throwing, I'd have more of a chance, but between Oaken and Wulfric, they'd picked, what was, obviously, my weakest area. It didn't help that every time he touched me, I quivered. What in Monsatsu's name was wrong with me? I was even beginning to annoy myself. Why couldn't Wulfric have partnered me with someone less damn good–looking? Someone with stringier arms or a less sculptured torso, or eyes that...

"Rose!" I came back to reality, cursing myself for getting lost in the cerulean hue. It was then I realised that this was the exact reason Wulfric had picked Oaken. It was nothing to do with his size. I was because he thought I was going to fall in love with him and act exactly like the girl he expected me to be. Well, I wasn't going to give him the satisfaction. I wasn't going to fall for him, I told myself firmly.

"You used that to your advantage when fighting me with that sword. There is no reason that you can't do the same again. Just pretend I have a sword in my hand, and you have yours. Do exactly what you did when you beat me."

"But I don't have my sword. It's over there," I pointed to the sword, next to where his lay.

"Rose, it wasn't the sword that beat me before. It was you. How did you do it? What were you thinking when you came at me?"

I thought back to when I'd rushed at him."

"I was mad at Wulfric for talking to me as if I was a little girl. I was angry that he called me Princess as though, that's all I was." I was also marvelling at the way the light caught his hair but I didn't tell him that part.

"Good. What else?"

"Then I thought of the dragon. You reminded me of him."

"Really?" He adopted a look I couldn't quite fathom. It made me feel embarrassed although I wasn't sure why.

"Come here and look at me,," Oaken demanded. It was pretty difficult as he stood at least a foot and a half taller. I had to look upwards. Those blue eyes looked down making me feel uncomfortable and some other feeling that I couldn't or didn't want to decipher.

"I'm a dragon. I've kidnapped a child, which I have here under my arm." He broke eye contact and ran to pick up a sandbag that was used for throwing practice. "The only thing between me getting away with this child is you. Remember how you felt when you were in that position yesterday. How you were the only one that could save those kids. Now think of how angry you were when Wulfric called you Princess and made you feel small."

"You did, too," I reminded him.

"Yes. How did you feel when I did that?"

"Angry."

"Good. Then if I remember rightly, you gave me a sewing project for tonight." He indicated the hole I'd made in his tunic. I could see his skin under the green fabric. It was bronzed as though he worked out in the fields with no top on. The thought made my cheeks burn. I hoped he thought my redness was from anger.

"Now focus all that anger and save this child." He gave a roar and ran at me. With only a tiny distance between us, I had little more than a few seconds to prepare for his attack. I ducked to the side and managed to miss him by millimetres. Quick as a flash, I turned and jumped onto his back. I could feel the hard bulk of his muscles beneath the thin green fabric. I couldn't hope to beat him on strength alone. I realised quickly that just holding onto him wasn't going to be enough. I had to think quickly before he realised where I was and pulled me off. I grabbed the top of his head and pulled backwards as hard as I could, all the while gripping his midriff with my thighs to make sure I didn't fall off. He was now looking straight up to the sky or would have been if my face wasn't there blocking it. I twisted his head to the side, and at the same time, he brought his right arm up to grab me. It was exactly what I'd anticipated he'd do. With only one hand free (the other was holding the sandbag), and with his head to the side, he was already at a disadvantage. I grabbed his right arm as it came up for me and used it to half-climb, half-jump up his body and then flip myself over to his other side. He was so disorientated that he didn't know where I was for a second, allowing me to grab the sandbag and make a dash for it. I'd never be able to hurt him in hand-to-hand combat. He was just too strong, and I was too small. But by using my advantage, I'd have more chance of getting away in a fight. At least, long enough to grab my sword. I had won by default, but it was good enough for me. I held the sandbag aloft and grinned. Surprisingly, he grinned back.

"Well done. You didn't technically beat me, but…"

"I got the sandbag, didn't I? I rescued the child." I did a little jig much to his amusement.

"You got lucky!"

"I seem to get lucky around you quite a lot!" I said it as a tease, but as soon as the words escaped my mouth, I realised just how it sounded. I could feel my cheeks flaming once again. "I meant that I have beaten you twice," I added lamely.

"You escaped from me. That's not the same. A win would have me on the ground with you on top of me."

If there was ever an answer that would have me feeling even more embarrassed, that was it. Was he still talking about combat or was he flirting with me? I was woefully inexperienced in the latter. To be honest, boys had never been a priority. I'd been more bothered about joining them in the arena than dating them. I left flirting and dating to the likes of Tarragon, who fell in love every other day and my elder sister Iris, who was undoubtedly the owner of the pink panties left in the kitchen just two days earlier.

"Let me show you some moves." Oaken moved towards me. A thrill of fear ran through me and without thinking, I stepped backwards, falling over both his and my swords. He laughed and raced towards me to help me up. This time, when he held his hand out, I took it. It felt rough, confirming what I already thought. He must have been a labourer of some kind, or a farmer. For the first time ever, I found myself really looking at a boy, a man really because there was no doubt he was over eighteen. The only boys I really knew were my brothers and some of the Club dignitaries' sons who attended school with me and none of them had the same presence as

Oaken. They looked nothing like him with their typical Club pale skin and muddy features. Oaken was tanned and had a head of thick sandy hair, another rarity in this kingdom.

"Are you a full on Club?" It was the rudest question that I could have asked, even surpassing in rudeness my remark to The Jack of Spades about his parents. Not for the first time, I wished I knew to keep my mouth shut or at the very least, think before I put it into gear.

Oaken only laughed.

"My mother is a shifter," he answered simply.

"You are half-Spade?" I questioned, pretty shocked. Mostly, the suits kept to their own kind, although as Tarragon had shown me earlier in the week, it wasn't completely unheard of for the suits to hook up with other suits.

"Actually, I'm not a Spade."

"I didn't mean to be rude. I'm sorry. I like the Spades, and I don't mind that you are half of one." I could do with a spade myself for the hole I was digging.

"I'm not offended, but that's not what I meant. I'm not a Spade. My mother came from a land of shifters way beyond the borders of Vanatus. She was from Gaelan."

"Wow!" I'd heard of other lands across the great ocean, but I'd never met anyone that had managed the journey from one to another. The sea was a cruel place, and only the bravest dared to fish there. Sea fish were an extremely rare commodity, usually only sold in the richest area of the Heart District and in some of the Diamondlands. I'd never even tasted sea fish. The few fishermen that lived in the Clublands lived in huge houses by the ocean. Many had tried to cross the ocean, but there was a whole history of Clubs and Spades who had perished attempting the feat.

"How did she get here?" I was genuinely curious to how she succeeded where everyone else failed.

"My father rescued her when she was a young woman. He's a fisherman like me."

Well, that explained the rugged appearance, huge muscular body, and tanned skin. He'd have to be strong, going out on a boat in the tempestuous ocean. It didn't explain how his mother got so close to the shore of Vanatus. Even the bravest fishermen and women didn't venture further out than the eye line of the coast.

"She set out on a huge boat. Apparently, Gaelan has much calmer waters than here, but as they got closer to Vanatus, the strong currents and stormy waters led to the boat sinking. Everyone on board drowned as the boat went down. My mother was the only survivor. She swam for days until she, too, almost perished from exhaustion, but my father saw her and pulled her out of the water. He said he fell instantly in love with her."

"How did she swim for so long?" The thought of swimming for days through the currents surrounding the Vanatus coastline was almost unbelievable.

"She's a mermaid shifter."

"What's a mermaid?" It wasn't a term I was familiar with.

"She can turn her bottom half into that of a fish."

I'd never heard of a fish shifter before. Birds and animals, yes, but never a sea creature.

"Just the bottom half?"

"Yes. Above the waist, she always looks like a woman. Below, she has either a fish tail or legs. It's been a long time since I've seen her shift, though. She tries to live like a Club as much as possible, although even without the scales, she still stands out, thanks to her blonde hair and blue eyes."

His story amazed me, and I couldn't help myself with the questions. My mother would throw a fit if she could hear how rude I was being.

"What animal do you shift into?"

"I can't. My mother's genes only went as far as me inheriting her colouring. I can't change into a fish or anything else."

"Doesn't that make your occupation a form of cannibalism?" I thought of him and his father bringing in a haul of fish. I wondered what his mother thought of it.

"She's not a fish." Oaken laughed. His pale hair tumbled over his eyes. He blew upwards to move it. He laughed so freely. Mostly at me it has to be said, but I was beginning to see a side of him that shone through the rough grunting exterior. I noticed dimples in his cheeks when his mouth creased upwards at the edges and the smile continued up into those blue eyes of his. It was mesmerising.

"She hasn't been down to the ocean since dad rescued her. I don't think she has any affinity with her scaly brethren. She prefers to live as a Club, and yes, she does sometimes eat fish with us."

I was certainly learning a lot about other people this week. It made me realise just how sheltered a life I led, stuck in the Castle all the time. It also made me thirsty to know more, to see more. I wanted nothing more at that moment than to meet Oaken's mother. Of course, I didn't say that to him. I'd suffered enough embarrassment in the last ten minutes.

"I've never eaten fish. What's it like?"

"You've never eaten fish? How is that possible?" a small furrow appeared between his eyes as he gazed at me with a look of almost confusion, as if he couldn't comprehend not having eaten fish before.

"What do you mean? Fish is really expensive. You should know that. You are the fisherman."

"Yeah, it's expensive, but you are a princess."

"We eat a lot of toadspawn stew at the castle."

Oaken scrunched up his nose in distaste. I tried not to notice just how cute the gesture looked on him.

"Some fish tastes better than others. We can fish Cod and Haddock reasonably easily, but they are nothing compared to the rainbowfish. If we are extremely lucky, we catch one or two a month. They are so rare that large ones can go for thousands."

"What do they taste like?" I'd never even heard of a rainbowfish before.

"I've only ever eaten rainbowfish once myself. We had amazing luck one time and managed to catch five rainbowfish in one haul. The chances of that happening are next to none, so it was an amazing achievement. We sold four of them and decided to eat the smallest. It was the most delicious meal I'd ever had in my life. It was over three years ago, and I can still remember the taste."

"What was it like?"

"Delicious, delectable, mouthwatering," he moved towards me, his eyes on mine. I found myself being unable to breathe again which, this time, had nothing to do with his body on me and everything to do with his eyes on mine. "Luscious, heavenly," he moved forward again so there was barely an inch between us. "every mouthful was a new experience, I devoured it as surely as I want to devour you right now".

I opened my mouth to say something, although I don't know what, when Wulfric shouted my name. Actually, he'd gone back to 'Princess', but I knew it was me he was talking to. I turned my head to look at him, acutely aware that my cheeks were now so red, there was no hiding them.

"Come over here. Your brother's a pro at archery. I want you partnered with him for the remainder of the session. Oaken, you can go over to the swordplay area. You could do with brushing up on your skills."

Oaken gave me an embarrassed smile and a wink as I left.

The rest of the session consisted of Sequoia shooting bullseyes on the huge targets and of me trying to do the same whilst sneakily looking past the target to see what Oaken was doing. He was brilliant with a sword. I don't know how I beat him. I began to wonder if he'd let me win?

I wasn't nearly as good as Sequoia at archery, but I hit the target more times than I missed it and even managed a couple of bullseyes myself. Not bad for a first attempt and the fact I couldn't keep my mind from wandering. When Wulfric called an end to the session, I dropped the bow and sheath of arrows into their container and rushed to the entrance. I wouldn't have admitted it to anyone, but I wanted to catch Oaken before he left. When I got to the big wooden gates, I watched the men leave, waiting for a mop of sandy hair amongst the brown heads. By the time Sequoia reached me with my sword, which I'd left behind, I realised that Oaken had already gone. A feeling engulfed me, one I wasn't familiar with. I felt somehow sad although I didn't know why. I knew it had nothing to do with the situation the country was in or my own part in that. It was something to do with the sandy-haired fisherman I'd only met for the first time just a couple of hours before.

"You did good today, kid." Sequoia ruffled my hair.

"Did I?"

"You should have heard Wulfric. He didn't know I was in earshot, but he was telling Arbor, he's the second in command here, that he'd never seen such potential in a new recruit. I was proud to be your brother out there today."

"Thanks, Sec. Do you think he'll go a bit easier on me now that he knows I can fight?"

"You're kidding, right? He'll work you harder *because* of the fact you can fight. You've let yourself in for a whole world of pain with him, kiddo. But you know what? You'll thank him for it when the time comes. He knows the situation, and he's building us all up to be ready for it. I wouldn't be surprised if he doubles or triples our workload. A couple of hours a day of training is nowhere near enough if there is a war coming.

"Do you really think it will come to that?"

"I have no doubt it will. It's been threatening for years. The Hearts want our water and control of The Diamond's mines. They charge so much for everything that it leaves the Clubs and the Spades poorer nations, and the Diamonds are so far removed from reality that they don't see how resentful their own people are at running the mines only to see the diamonds going straight into the hands of The Hearts. The Spades are on the verge of a civil war of their own, and the royal family isn't doing anything about it. The King is a complete mess, at the moment, and who knows where the Queen is. The economy is a mess, and there are a lot of very unhappy people. I think Father has known for years how fragile everything was, but he, along with the other ruling families, continued the charade of New Years Eve Parties, as if the people care that their royal families have a good new year or not. I guess we'll find out just how fixable it all is when Father calls us all together. I think he'll do that tonight.

It turned out that Sequoia was wrong. By the time I fell into bed that night, I'd not been summoned to my father, and as I'd heard nothing from my brothers and sisters, I assumed they hadn't either. They wouldn't leave me out of something as important as my own future.

It was with a heavy heart that I fell onto my bed. I still didn't know what would happen to me, and with the death sentence hanging over me, sleep was not going to come easily. Then a flicker of light ran through my conscious. No, not light but sandy, almost golden hair. For some inexplicable reason, I was thinking about Oaken and just the thought of the feel of his muscles under his light tunic made me fall asleep with a smile on my lips.

January 4th

I woke up to the sound of an urgent rapping on my door.

"Come in," I said sleepily, imagining it to be Star. I was quite surprised to see Tree standing there, although not as surprised as him to find me still in my nightclothes.

"Um, sorry, Ma'am. The King would like to see you."

"About time!" I jumped out of bed causing Tree to turn bright red. Realising I was making him uncomfortable, I told him to tell my Father I'd be down in five minutes, allowing him to leave. It was not customary for the male members of the household staff to be in a princess' bedchambers. Poor Tree.

I pulled on the first thing I could find in my wardrobe, an old hand-me-down dress that had once belonged to Star, and threw it over my head.

I found my father, not in the huge family sitting room with the rest of the royal family, but in his study alone.

The window was open, and a slight breeze caught the door behind me making it bang.

"Sorry, Father." I gave a customary curtsey and sat at the only other seat in the room. Behind my Father, I saw the first flurry of snow this winter, cascading down past the window.

"No matter, child. I'm sorry to have not come to you last night, but I was up until the early hours talking to a load of idiots who seem to think war will be in the best interests of our nation." His voice was gruff, but his manner was anything but. "About this death sentence that the bloody Hearts have you up for. I've put in an appeal because, to be honest, it's a load of bloody nonsense, and they know it. If they don't hire nannies with an ounce of common sense, what the blazes do they expect to happen? Your appeal is on the sixth in two day's time. I tried to get them to consider it earlier, but, apparently, the whole world has gone to pot because one woman couldn't keep her knickers on, and another is a raving maniac."

I had to stifle a giggle at the way he spoke about the other Royal Queens. No one else would have gotten away with it. I sorely doubted he'd get away with it if he spoke like that in any other company but his own family. He pulled out his pipe and filled it with tobacco. Putting it in his mouth, he rummaged around in his drawer before turning to me.

"I don't suppose you have a light do you? No, of course, you don't. Blazes! I could do with that bally dragon of yours here now."

"He wasn't my dragon father. He was a Spade."

"Yes, yes, dragon, Spade, whatever. He'd still be useful now to light my bloody pipe."

I hoped he'd been more eloquent when putting my case forward for appeal. When the time came, I'd ask Sage to talk on my behalf.

"Would you like me to find you a light, Daddy?"

"No," he said, dropping his pipe onto the desk where the clump of tobacco fell out. "No need. I probably should quit anyway. Your mother keeps on at me. Now where was I?"

"The appeal on the sixth."

"Ah, yes. I'll have to take you up to the Aces palace in Urbis. The grand court is there, and the Hearts have forced me to push it all the way to the top."

Although I'd rather have had it dealt with in a court in the Clublands, this was not entirely unexpected,. With the other suits in play, I knew that option was not likely.

"What do you think they will do?"

"It all depends on which Ace you get. The Ace of Clubs would be your best bet because at the end of the day he's one of us. Plus, he's a little bit soft in the head, which might help. The Diamond is firm but fair, the Spade only comes to hearings when he's forced to so I have no idea what he's like, and the Heart, well, she's just like all the other Hearts. Probably best if we don't get her."

"It all sounds rather biased."

"Isn't everything? Don't worry, though. Even the Ace of Hearts should be able to see that common sense prevails. You'll get a fair trial. Until then, I've been told to keep you in the castle."

"Mother already told me last night."

"I heard you went out to the training grounds," he said, changing the subject.

"Yes, but they are on the grounds of the castle. Mother said it was ok."

"She was wrong. You have to stay within the castle itself."

"But, but. I only just started my training." A flash of sandy hair ran through my mind once more. I tried not to think about it.

"It won't do you any good now anyway. I'm seeing Wulfric after you. The bloody Hearts have been trampling all over the mountainous regions of the Clublands, pretending they are after the dragons when we all know they want to divert the spring water so it runs through their land. I wouldn't mind, but I've had reports that they are destroying people's homes in the process and using what's left to help themselves. I'm sending Wulfric out with his men this morning to stop them."

"Will there be fighting?"

"I should imagine so, although I'd prefer there not be."

"So let me go fight. I'm one of Wulfric's men now." I drew myself up to my full height, which wasn't very much and tried to look as strong as the men I'd been in the arena with yesterday. He wasn't buying it.

"You'll stay in the castle until the sixth as I've already told you and don't be getting any ideas about running away from home to join the troops. I've got enough to contend with at the moment without adding a wayward daughter to my problems."

"Yes, Daddy." Romantic thoughts of nights under the stars with Oaken on the way to battle quickly evaporated.

I dismissed myself and walked glumly back to my room. I'd been so excited about warrior training and, if I was going to be honest with myself, seeing Oaken again. He'd occupied my thoughts almost completely for the past twenty-four hours, and as everything else was so terrible to think about, Oaken was the only positive part of what was shaping up to be the worst week of my life.

I watched from my bedroom window as they all marched past it and out of the castle gates, all kitted out for battle. Even from this distance, I spotted Oaken amongst a sea of brown-haired boys. I wanted nothing more than to be down there with them, but I couldn't disobey my father. He was right. He had enough going on without worrying about me. My three eldest brothers had gone out into battle and even though the likelihood was that they'd come back without injury, hopefully after talking sense into the Hearts, there was no guarantee. I spent the rest of the day in my room. Tree graciously brought my meals up for me, although I noticed he wouldn't catch my eyes as he did.

The night was filled with bloody dreams

January 5th

The snow swirled around my window, a blizzard, heavier than any I'd seen in previous years. It followed the general mood around the castle. I'd found my mother crying, and I didn't have to ask why. Three of her sons had gone to fight, and the weather was against them. In fact, the weather was a bigger enemy than the Hearts. It was impossible to know just how many Hearts were up in the mountains, but my father had intelligence that there weren't that many and that they were way outnumbered by our own troops. Of course, he could have been saying that for our mother's benefit.

I decided to leave my room and spend time with my family. For the first time in days, I ate with them as opposed to having meals in my room. Without my brothers there, the banquet room seemed eerily empty, even though there were still nine of us around the table. The sombre mood was like an infestation, and even the staff looked subdued as they brought out food to us. There had been no news brought back overnight, and even Father didn't know how things were going. Apparently, there were conflicting reports coming in from his various advisors, and the newspapers didn't help matters. The Club Gazette had been told to keep out any information about our troops heading up to the mountains, but this morning's edition still managed to have photos of Wulfric and his men preparing for battle. Headlines including words such as 'bravery' and 'courage' filled the pages. Had a stranger come into town, they would have thought that The Clubs were a race of brave warriors fighting to clear the name of their wronged princess. That would be me then. Someone had managed to secure a subscription to the other three newspapers, and we even had today's Diamond Times. I featured heavily, still, on the front page of the Heart Echo although most of the paper was taken up with how the dragon had gone crazy because of our magic water, and they were going to do something about it. The spin they had put on the story was amazing. Did the Hearts think that their subjects would be so stupid as to forget that the dragon was actually a shifter? The Spade Chronicle mainly consisted of reports of unconfirmed sightings of their Queen, and the Diamond Times painted a very broad and vague overview of what was happening in all four kingdoms.

The day dragged by slowly, and each hour the snow got heavier and heavier. Nobody mentioned the men out in the cold, but I did catch my mother crying on more than one occasion when she thought no one was looking. My father locked himself in his huge defence room, a large room in the basement of the castle that consisted of a massive 3D plan of the whole of Clubland, maps of Vanatus and the other kingdoms within it, and a huge detailed street map of Urbis complete with street names and shops carefully labelled. His high-ranking intelligence officers congregated down there with him. Between the worry about my brothers and the fragile state of the kingdom, my court date tomorrow seemed to have been forgotten by everyone except me. It was almost as though the fact I had the threat of a death sentence hanging over my head was not as important as everything else going on. Normally, in situations like this, I'd tell myself not to be so self-centred, but damn it, it was my life we were talking about. After dinner, from which my father was absent, and my mother cried through, I decided to go back up to my room and watch through the window for any sign of Wulfric and his men returning.

I watched the garden where the doe and her fawn had returned. Someone was feeding them, and on closer inspection, I saw that it was Star. Only Star would go out on a day as cold as this to feed the wildlife. The fawn would probably die without Star's help, though, as it could barely see over the top of the snow. I could see her moving towards the fawn now, and I had to crane my neck to see exactly what she was doing. At first, it looked like she was going to capture it; but instead, she placed a blanket on the tiny thing. As I watched, though, I saw that I'd been right the first time. She had actually picked the tiny fawn up and was carrying him out of the garden. Surprisingly, the doe followed but without trying to get her fawn back. The whole situation was weird. Star loved animals and had a menagerie of them, but she harped on so much about wild animals being allowed to stay in the wild that it was strange to see her messing with nature.

When she came to my room half an hour later, the fawn was the only thing on my mind.

"Hey, Rose. I came to see how you were doing and bring you this. It's for your court appearance."

She had a navy blue dress with red piping and white collar draped over her arm. It was both pretty and smart at the same time. I thanked her and placed it on the bed.

"What were you doing in the garden? I saw you pick up a fawn."

"I didn't want to do it, but he was born so early. Usually, fawns are born in spring. It's been unseasonably warm of late so I hoped the little guy would be ok, but with this weather, he wouldn't survive. I had to take him, or he would have died. The doe knows me. She knew I wouldn't harm her baby. They are both cosy and warm in the animal shed. I'll let them both out as soon as this snow melts.

"I don't think that's going to happen anytime soon. The Diamond Times has forecast heavy snow for the next three weeks, at least."

"The Diamonds were the only ones that could accurately forecast the weather. They used some kind of meteorogical spell or something and printed the results in the paper. The Spades were pretty good at reading weather patterns, but only for about twenty-four hours ahead. The Clubs looked up if they wanted to know what the weather was like. If you were wet, it was raining; if you were cold and white, it was snowing. We weren't known for being the most technological of races.

"Will he survive?"

"I hope so. I've made him comfortable and given him food. Both he and the doe are eating, which is a good sign."

"What are you going to name him?" I asked sitting on the bed.

"Rose, please stop talking about the deer. I know you are worried about tomorrow, but you've not talked about it all day."

"How could I talk about it? Sage, Sequoia, and Ash are knee deep in snow fighting the Hearts. Mother won't stop crying. Father is nowhere to be seen, and war looks like it's going to happen. No one cares about me." Even as I said it, I was aware I was whining, but I felt like whining. Star was the first person I'd talked to all day.

"Rose, you know that's not true. We all care about you; it's just that..." she trailed off.

"It's just that everyone is too busy to notice."

"We are all worried about the boys. It doesn't mean we are not worried about you, too. Tarragon is in with mother right now writing your defence."

"Really?" I wasn't exactly sure I wanted Tarragon writing my defence; in fact, I wasn't even sure he could spell the word defence, but I was touched at the thought. Star came up and put her arm around my shoulder.

"I asked Father if I could come with you tomorrow, but, apparently, you are only allowed to have one person with you. He asked me to tell you to be ready for seven am. The hearing is at eleven. He's ordered private transport for you both."

"What private transport?" The shire horses were used for local transport, and we did have a carriage for longer journeys to Urbis. I had thought we would be taking this.

"Are we not going by carriage?"

"Apparently, the snow is too deep for the horses."

"Oh." I guess I'd see what we were travelling in tomorrow. It didn't really matter as long as I got there on time.

"Wear the dress. It's smart. If you like, I can come and braid your hair in the morning."

"Thank you, Star." I hugged her closely. "I think I'd rather not see anyone tomorrow. I'm going to be nervous enough as it is."

We both knew that this might be the last time we saw each other. If I was convicted and handed the death sentence, I'd not be allowed to come home to say goodbye. The Aces were pretty quick in matters as serious as this. If I was found guilty, I would be hung within the week.

There were tears in Star's eyes as she left, but she managed to hold her composure long enough to close the door behind her without bursting into tears. She did a better job than I. The second the door closed, tears started falling down my own face, and I thought I heard quiet sobbing coming from behind the door. It subsided as she walked away and down the corridor.

I held up the dress and hung it up to keep it uncreased. I might be going to my death tomorrow, but I was going to do it smartly and with a little pride and dignity.

January 6th

I had hoped that my breakfast would be brought to me in my room, and I could just slip out of the castle unseen. But my mother woke me up at five along with all my remaining brothers and sisters. They brought me down to the banquet hall where the biggest breakfast I'd ever seen was waiting for me. I know they had organised it to make me feel better, but to me, it felt like it was a last meal. I only forced some food down to spare their feelings. I'd never felt less hungry in my life. When the time came for me to leave, everyone was in tears. It alleviated my fears that no one cared about me. I was grateful to have such a wonderful family, but I just wanted to be gone. It was unbearable seeing them crying, wondering if I'd ever see them again. My father opened the door, and I was surprised to be told that we were walking to our transport. That ruled out the dirigible. It was at least a fifteen-minute horse ride to the station. We'd never make it on foot in this weather. The snow had stopped falling, and the sky was clear, but snow still covered the ground like a thick white blanket. Instead of heading out towards the local town, we turned towards the field at the side of the castle. When I turned the corner, I finally understood how we were going to get to Urbis so quickly. A huge, brightly coloured, hot air balloon stood in the centre of the snow covered field ready to go. Four ropes tied to the ground held it down, and two men stood in the basket waiting for us. Another stood in front of the basket, and when I got closer, I saw it was Tree. He bowed as we got closer and opened a kind of gate in the front of the basket.

Two days ago, I'd have been terrified of getting in something that flew so high in the air, but after chasing a dragon on what was, basically, a flying horse, I figured there wasn't much difference. When my father got into the tiny basket beside me and closed the wicker gate, one of the men in there with us pressed something that made a huge whoosh of flame fly right up inside the balloon and lifted us up off the ground. Tree quickly undid the ropes that were tethering us to the ground, and we began to climb. Another whoosh of flame took us higher still, and it was only a few seconds before we cleared the treetops. The height of the balloon and the flame so close to where I was, ironically, reminded me of the dragon and the last time I'd made this particular journey. At least, this time, the flame was above me, and the jets were positioned so they were pointing upwards. I didn't have to worry about being roasted to death.

As we flew over the castle, I searched the distant terrain to see if I could spot our troops returning. I thought I might have seen a group of men for a split second, but they were so far away, and we were heading away from the mountains towards Urbis. My mind kept wandering back to Oaken, no matter how much I tried to think about something else. I wondered how they were all doing and if they'd managed to stop the Hearts peacefully or had to use force. I knew there was no point fretting about the boys when I had my own, very large problem to sort out, but images of wounded men and blood-splattered battlefields kept creeping into my brain, no matter what I did to stop them. I tried looking over the side of the basket to take my mind off it. The journey was largely boring and took so much longer than it had on Elphin. Below us, I spotted fields of livestock. Cows, the size of ants and sheep so small, I could barely see them. Every so often, I spotted clumps of houses and tiny villages. After a while, I brought my attention to the balloon itself. It seemed to be made from swathes of gold and red fabric held together by a series of interconnecting ropes and the thing that powered the flame was really no more than an oversized brass gas lamp. It was undoubtedly a Heart invention. None of the other suits had the engineering capacity to come up with something so amazing. Despite my general mistrust of the Hearts, they certainly came up with some ingenious ideas and had the technical ability to turn them into reality. There was no way in a million years a Club would have been able to think up such a wonderful idea.

Eventually, four spires appeared on the horizon, the Aces Palace and the venue of my trial today. As we got closer, the little specks in front of the spires turned into houses and the bustling city of Urbis.

The man turned something on a dial, and the jets of heat got smaller. The balloon began to descend, and we hit the ground in the same field all the Urbisites had congregated in just days before right outside the huge iron gates that marked the entrance to Urbis. The field was now empty save for one or two people making their way to the city gates and a couple of horses who were searching for grass in the snow.

I thanked the balloon owner (who was a Club despite his balloon not being) and followed my father through the entranceway to Urbis. The long straight road up to the imposing palace was quieter than I'd ever seen it. To the left of it, ran the wall that separated Cerce from The Club District, so it was impossible to know how busy it was in there. But to the right, The Club District looked almost deserted. Smoke poured out of hundreds of little chimneys, showing that people were keeping warm at home rather than braving the frigid weather, or perhaps, they were afraid of another rampaging dragon. As we got closer to the Palace, the quaint thatched cottages thinned out making way for the commercial part of the district. Despite the fact it was literally right next to Cerce, it was a million miles away in style. There were no alleyways of expensive shops selling state of the art gadgets and designer shoes. All we had was a huge outdoor marketplace, each stall covered with a different coloured umbrella. These umbrellas were not the pretty parasols that were sold in boutiques in Cerce but huge dyed raffia ones. Brilliant for keeping out the sun, not so great for keeping out the rain in the heavy downpours. I would have loved to have seen the rainbow of colours from the sky. It was a shame we hadn't flown over them in the balloon. The Club District market was one of my favourite places. Usually, a hive of activity with hundreds of amazing smells and sights, selling everything from spices to clothes. Today, however, whether due to the political climate or the actual climate, there were only a few of the stalls set up and even fewer shoppers browsing. As we walked past, one of the stall owners closed his stall, tutting as he did so.

Urbis was so huge that it took a full twenty minutes at a brisk walking pace to get to the palace. Usually, we would have hired a horse and carriage to take us from the entrance, but, just like all the other businesses, there were no horses there to hire. The palace itself was in the centre of Urbis in the one part of the big city that wasn't owned by one suit. Inner Urbis was open to all and included the Urbis University and other government buildings.

The palace loomed taller than any building I'd ever seen and was probably the largest in all of Vanatus. The huge gold doors at the front of the white stone building stood at least three storeys high by themselves. Two guards stood at either side of the open doors, each wearing the uniform of the Palace. You could tell a member of the Ace Palace staff by what he or she wore. The uniform consisted of a tunic with four rectangles, two black and two red, each with the emblem of each suit embroidered in gold thread, with gold trim around the cuffs and collar. They wore black trousers with gold piping down the side of each leg and black shoes with a square gold buckle on the front.

They nodded as we passed and I walked into the biggest room I'd ever seen. The huge room was technically an atrium and had light flooding in through massive skylights. Everywhere was white, from the white marble floor to the huge staircase that ran upwards at the end of the atrium. Red carpets with gold edges ran to both the left and right and the seal of Urbis was inlaid into the marble floor in gold. The most breathtaking part was the back wall. It had a cascade of water falling down along the full length of it. The water emerged from the top of the hundred or so foot tall wall and then disappeared into the ground. I could only assume there was some kind of hidden grate as the floor was completely dry. In front of the waterfall was a desk with a sign saying reception. A woman wearing a smart white dress with the four suit logos discreetly embroidered on the breast pocket in gold thread greeted us.

"Hello, welcome to Ace Palace. How may I help you today, your highnesses?" She was good. I'd never met her before, but she knew exactly who I was. Perhaps it was in the palace training to know all the royals and dignitaries of Vanatus. She smiled a sincere smile with red-coated lips. Although it was difficult to tell without all the unnecessary pomp that usually surrounded them, I thought she might be a Heart. If she did have the gold tattoos that the hearts usually wore, they were discreetly covered. Of course, I could have been wrong, and she could have been a Diamond or a Spade.

"We are here for a hearing at the court."

"Of course," she ruffled through some papers on a clipboard she was holding.

"You are in Court Number One. I'll have Jenny show you the way." She nodded her head almost imperceptibly, and a young palace worker appeared as if from nowhere.

"Jenny, would you you show His Royal Highness, the King of Clubs and Her Royal Highness, Lady Rose, the Two of Clubs to Court One, please."

"I'd be delighted. If you'd just follow me this way." She set off walking along the red carpet, and we followed right behind her. She took us to the waterfall and just as I thought I was about to get wet, it parted like a curtain to reveal a door. It was then that I realised that the waterfall was nothing but an illusion. It wasn't the great engineering of The Hearts that had developed it but the magic of The Diamonds or possibly one of the Aces themselves. The door was marked 'Courts 1 to 5', which took us to a long red-carpeted corridor. We passed four doors, two on the right and two on the left. The ones on the right had the numbers five and three on them whereas the ones on the left were marked with four and two. The door right at the end of the corridor had the number one above it.

"A little trivia for you," the girl said, "Court Number One is both the oldest and largest of all ten courtrooms in the palace. It's reserved for the most important cases and can hold up to two thousand people. It has only been filled to capacity twice since it was built. The first was in..."

"Excuse me," I butted in. However much I liked the building, I wasn't here for a history lesson. "Can you tell me which Ace is taking the trial."

"Oh, I'm sorry. I don't know. The Aces very rarely take trials these days. Usually, one of our many high court judges steps in for them."

"It will be an Ace at this trial," my father said as the door opened and another uniformed worker opened the door and bade us welcome.

"Good luck," said Jenny as she turned to leave us. I wondered briefly if she had thought 'you're going to need it'.

When we walked into the room, we were greeted by a young man, who was definitely a Spade, (a goat shifter, judging by his rectangular pupils). He showed me to a raised podium next to the judge's desk and my father to a gallery seating area. I was thankful that the court was almost empty despite it being the biggest in Urbis. A huge balcony curved round three of the walls and every single seat in it was empty. A few people sat in the same area as my father, and judging by their notepads, they were reporters. Apart from that, there was only the young man who had shown us to our seats and a seated woman in spectacles with a large drawing book of blank pages and a set of different width charcoals. Almost as soon as I stood on the podium, she picked up one of the charcoal pieces and began to sketch. Even though from where I was positioned, I couldn't see what she was drawing, I could tell from the way she was looking at me that I was her subject. I didn't really care about her, though. My eyes were fixed on the door to my right from whence the Ace would enter. I remembered what my father had told me and crossed my fingers behind my back, all the while praying to Monsatsu for the Club Ace to walk through it.

A noise to my right made me turn the other way, and a group of twelve people trooped in and sat in a separate section. The Jury. These men and women, along with the Ace, would decide in the next few hours if I lived or died. I couldn't tell with all of them but there looked to be a fair cross section of suits. The Clubs were obvious, they were all tiny compared to the others, and if that didn't give it away, the pointed ears would. There were three of them, two men and a woman. The other nine people were much harder to place, but one woman with bright pink lipstick and gold eyeliner was obviously a Heart, even if she was dressed in the same red and black robes as the others. They were probably made to dress the same so there was no cheating. I was willing to bet that there were three of each suit. As I was just trying to figure out if one of the men was a Diamond or Heart, the judge's door behind me opened. I turned and held my breath, hoping for the Ace of Clubs. I wasn't in luck. There was only one female Ace, and as this was a woman, it meant only one thing. She was the Ace of Hearts. My heart dropped at roughly the same time as my stomach rose to meet it. I had to swallow a few times not to be sick. What had my father said?

'Probably best if we don't get The Ace of Hearts.' The thought that I might actually be convicted of murder suddenly got a lot more real. She was a large woman, and although she didn't look mean, as such (as the Queen of Hearts did), she hardly looked like a dear old granny either. Her steel grey hair was tied in a bun, and she wore ceremonial judge's robes with only her crest on them, a tiny heart in gold embroidery.

"You may be seated," she said as she took her own place. I looked behind me for a seat, but there wasn't one. It was then that I realised that everyone else had stood up as she entered and were now beginning to sit down. I guess potential convicts weren't allowed the luxury of seating, and I'd have to stand throughout the hearing.

The young man who had ushered us in turned out to be more than just a doorman. He had taken a position in the centre of the courtroom and now addressed the Ace.

"Your Honour, ladies, gentlemen," he turned slightly to acknowledge the jury. "We are gathered here for the trial of Lady Rose Club, otherwise known as The Two of Clubs. On Sunday, the first of January, she was seen following a gentleman by the name of Drage Fortis to Cerce where she was seen by a witness to first steal a flame gun from the well-known shop, Clockwork. She then proceeded to use said flame gun to murder Mr. Fortis."

"That's not what happened at all!" I shouted across at him. How on earth was I going to get a fair trial if he told everyone what happened like that? He'd not even mentioned that Drage Fortis was a dragon shifter. I saw my father put his head in his hands.

"Lady Club," the Ace began. Her steel-coloured hair matched her eyes perfectly, I noticed as she pointed them in my direction. "I will forgive you your outburst as you probably haven't been versed on courtroom decorum, but in my court, you will only speak when you are spoken to. Any more outbursts from you, however, and I will be forced to convict you without a trial. Do you understand me?"

"Yes, your honour," I said and wondered if I'd even get a chance to speak again.

"Now," she continued, turning to the man in the centre. "You said there was a witness."

"That's correct, Your Honour, a Mr. Pike. He is a photographer for the Heart Echo and just happened to be in Cerce when the incident occurred. I'll call him now, but as we are waiting, you may wish to look at the photos he took of the incident." He passed a brown envelope to the Ace, who opened it and peered at its contents. I tried to crane my neck to see the photos, but she had them angled away from me so I couldn't see them. When she was done, she passed them back to, what was evidently, the prosecutor, who handed them to the jury. I watched in frustration as they passed the photos around. Whilst all this was going on, a man had been brought in. A small nervous-looking man, whom I would have taken for a rat or ferret shifter had he not been wearing the most ridiculous outfit. Only a Heart would wear something with so many frills.

"Can you state your name for the court?" The Ace asked once the man had been put in his rightful position within the courtroom.

"Furittus Pike, your honour."

"Occupation?"

"I work for ver Echo." He appeared nervous, and in between answering the Ace's questions, he gazed around the room as if he was expecting to be convicted himself. I wondered what illegal activities he'd been up to. He looked the type to have been up to no good. His accent was that of the street and thus almost impossible to understand.

"Suit?"

"I'm a Spade, Your Honour."

Well, there was a surprise. He looked like a shifter, but those clothes were all Heart.

"So what were you doing in Cerce on January the first, Mr. Pike."

"I live vere, don't I?"

"Is that a question, Mr. Pike? You don't seem very sure."

"I am sure, and, no, it wasn't a question. I live in Cerce. Have done for ver past five years." He scratched behind his ears and looked at the ground. I'd bet my last penny he was a rat or ferret shifter. I wondered why he had to state his suit. It had nothing to do with the case, so why even mention it? I'm a proud Club, but some people like to hide their suits. It looked like Mr.

Pike was doing his very best to fit in with the Hearts, although he was a very long way from matching their good looks and charm. It was then that I realised I'd been doing the exact same thing all day. I'd labelled the man who took us in the balloon a Club before even speaking to him. I'd painted the woman at the reception desk a Heart. I'd even done it with the jury, mentally sorting them into suits. It began to dawn on me that I was actually part of the problem, and I wasn't talking about murdering anyone. I'd spent my whole life labelling people. If they were pretty, they were a Heart, fast, a Spade, nature-loving, a Club. The truth was, there were beautiful, fast, nature-lovers in all suits, just like the other stereotypical characteristics of each suit could really belong to anyone. I suddenly felt more ashamed than I had in my whole life.

"Can you tell us," began the Ace, "What exactly you saw on the first of January."

"Well, ver fing is, I was on my way to an assignment wiv my camera and vis big dragon appeared out of nowhere. At first, I fink people were interested like, but ven 'e started jumping around all over ver place."

"Did you see what caused this change in the dragon?"

"Not at first. Ev'ryone was getting scared, and vere was people running about and screaming. I 'id in a 'ouse until it quietened down a bit. When I looked out ver winder, vere she was on a flyin' 'orse. She 'ad a flame gun. She hit 'im and ven flew to ver ground to catch ver kiddies like."

"Excuse me, Mr. Pike. Are you telling me there were children present?" The Ace looked quite confused. She wasn't the only one.

"Yeah, course. The royal kiddies. One ov your lot and a Spade. She caught vem when the dragon let go."

"So the dragon had the children?"

"I just said vat din I? He 'ad ver kiddies, and ven he dropped em when she flamed 'im

"Where was Mr. Fortis when all this was going on?"

"I just said! He dropped ver kiddies. Blimey."

Now they both seemed frustrated with each other. The most apparent thing about the Ace's questions was that no one had briefed her and that she didn't read the newspapers. My chances of getting out of here were looking slimmer and slimmer. I started to bite my nails if only to keep myself from shouting out about the injustice of it all.

"The Dragon was Mr. Fortis, your honour," the prosecutor explained much to the relief of Mr Pike who was nodding his head furiously , "He was a dragon shifter."

"Ah, I see, and can you explain to me what he was doing with the children."

"As far as I'm aware," continued the prosicutor "he flew into the Club Castle when they were holding a party for all the royal families and took three royal children. He then flew to Urbis with them. Lady Club followed him and got the children."

"It sounds to me as though Lady Club actually set out to save the children, would you not say?"

"Well, yes, Your Honour, but the fact remains, she still murdered a man."

"D'yer still need me like, or can I be off like?" Furittus shuffled around on the spot and wrung his hands.

"You shall remain, Mr. Pike," replied the judge before turning to me. I finally got the feeling that I might actually get a fair hearing after all.

"Can you tell the court your version of events, Lady Club?"

Finally! I was being allowed to speak. I'd been worried that I'd not get the chance. I cleared my throat and began, trying to sound as clear and polite as possible.

"I felt a bit ill during my family's party, so I was getting a bit of fresh air on the grounds. A dragon flew in and took the two youngest members of the Spade Royal Family and the Youngest of the Heart Royal Family. I borrowed a winged unicorn and followed him to Urbis. I did take the flame gun, and I did hit the dragon with it, but I didn't know he was a Spade. There is a colony of real dragons up in the mountains of The Clublands, and I just assumed that it was one of those. Once I'd rescued the children from him, I went to check on the dragon, but all I found was an injured man. I didn't even realise that it was the dragon, who had shifted back to a Spade persona. I thought he was a man who had been burned by the dragon. I tried to save his life, but it was already too late. He died in my arms."

"Is this what Happened, Mr. Pike?"

"Could've, I spose. I only saw 'er wiv ver dead man."

"Did it look like she was trying to save his life?"

"She was 'oldin' 'is 'ead and talkin' to 'im. I fink she might've been tellin' 'im to 'old on."

"Hmmm. You are dismissed Mr. Pike." Furittus rushed out of the court as quickly as he could manage and the Ace turned to me.

"Why, I wonder, did you decide to attack the dragon? If what you say is true, surely you would have just followed him until he landed safely. That course of action would have been much less risky to the children, would it not?"

"That's what I had set out to do, Your Honour, but when I caught up with him, he was rampaging around Cerce. He had already destroyed some buildings. Before he had even got to Urbis, he had dropped one of the children. I saved her and took her to my old nanny's house in the Club District before I carried on to look for the dragon. When I did catch up with him, some Diamonds were shooting spells at him from their side of the wall. I think that was what made him go crazy. Most of the people of Urbis evacuated."

"Did they?"

She probably never left the Palace. I wondered how someone so completely out of touch could be expected to be a judge. Perhaps not knowing anything kept her impartial.

"They did, your honour. Most of the streets were empty. When I saw the Diamonds begin to load a trebuchet, I worried that they would accidentally hurt the children so I used the flame gun on him."

"Weren't you worried that the flame thrower would hurt the children?"

"Yes, Your Honour, but I aimed for his wings. I only wanted to startle him, not really hurt him, but the flame gun was more powerful that I had realised. I actually didn't know it was a flame gun until I pressed the trigger, and by then, it was too late. I'd hit him. I had to catch the children before they hit the ground, but once they were safe, I went to check on the dragon, which is when I found Mr. Fortis lying on the ground with what I assumed at the time to be dragon burns. It wasn't until the next morning when I saw Mr. Furittus's photos and the accompianing article in the papers that I realised that I had caused those burns."

"Hmm. It seems to me that it was very much a case of mistaken identity. I'm quite baffled to understand why we have been called here to hear a case of murder when it seems we should, instead, be here to reward you for your bravery."

I couldn't believe what I was hearing. I was going to be acquitted?

"Preposterous!" A woman I'd not noticed in the seating area stood up. When I looked at her closely, I realised it was The Queen of Hearts. "If it hadn't been for her, my city wouldn't be ruined. She admits herself that she murdered the man and destroyed my favourite shoe shop to boot."

"The shoe shop was hit by a boulder laced with magic," I replied, "The Diamonds did that."

"Silence!" yelled the Ace. "Your Highness, it's customary to be invited to the court if you wish to speak. You should have made an application before the trial started. You cannot speak from the public gallery."

"This girl murdered a man in my District. I'm the Queen of that district, and I'll talk wherever I want to."

"May I remind you that even royalty are bound by the laws of this land, and if you speak out of term again, I will hold you in contempt of court and have you taken to a holding cell. Furthermore, it sounds like Lady Club here saved your child's life. If anyone should be giving her credit, it should be you. I'm not going to force you to apologise, but I would think, the royals should set an example to their subjects in every way."

"They shouldn't have let a dragon take my child in the first place!" squealed the Queen in anger. "I want the whole Club Royal family brought to court on endangerment charges and the Diamonds too for wilful destruction!"

"I may be powerful, but even I cannot bring a whole country to court," replied the Ace "I am ashamed to be a Heart right now, but you leave me no choice. Guards, please take The Queen to a holding cell."

A Couple of guards stood. Both looked afraid. I wasn't surprised. I wouldn't have liked to get caught between the Queen of Hearts and the Ace of Hearts. Both were formidable women.

"Don't bother, I'm leaving!" huffed The Queen. I couldn't help myself; I cracked out a grin just as the Queen's face turned cherry red with anger. I was willing to bet no one had put her in her place quite so publicly before. She gave me the most evil look before flouncing out of the courtroom and slamming the door with a bang behind her. The guards looked to the Ace for guidance, but she just gave her head a small shake. Both men looked relieved and sat back in their places.

"I cannot make a decision about whether Lady Club is guilty or not guilty. That is your job," she addressed the jury. "I will give you time to come to a verdict. We will meet back here in one hour, precisely. Lady Club, you are free to leave the courtroom, but you must not leave the palace. I want you back here when the jury returns."

"Yes, your honour." The jury filed out and left through a door at the side of the courtroom. I joined my father, and, together, we left through the door we came in through. Jenny was waiting for us.

"I've been asked to escort you to the cafeteria. We serve coffee and cakes there, and I thought you might like a break before you have to go back in. How did it go?"

A flash went off to my right, and I saw that the journalists and photographers had followed us. I guessed they weren't allowed to use photography in the courtroom, but they were making up for it out here. A reporter shoved a microphone under my nose and asked me how I felt about the murder.

"Would you be able to provide somewhere more private?" I heard my father asking Jenny.

"Come with me." Jenny smiled.

My father and I followed Jenny, and the reporters followed us. We ended up in the large atrium where the waterfall had been transformed into a jungle scene complete with animals and birds. I didn't have time to take it all in as Jenny was now whisking us toward another door. She almost pushed us through it, and as she shut the door behind us, I heard her tell the journalists that it was a restricted part of The Palace, and they would have to wait to get more photographs.

When I looked around the room she had pushed us into, I saw that it was actually the Palace kitchen. A chef dressed in all whites looked at us quizzically as we ran through. A door at the other end of the kitchen led out into the public cafeteria. A few people were eating, but none of them looked up and paid any attention to us. I sat at a table and picked up a menu.

"What the blazes just happened? I asked for somewhere private, and she shoved us into a kitchen," my father asked.

"She's a genius. The reporters are going to be standing at the kitchen door for the next hour waiting for us to come out. They probably think it's a private room. In the meantime, we can have a cup of tea in peace. I don't know about you, but I could really eat a piece of that delicious looking cake over there."

My father grinned as he realised what I was saying was true. I matched his grin. Things were looking up and for the first time in nearly a week, I felt that I could finally put an end to this madness. Yes, I'd technically killed a man. That would haunt me for the rest of my life, but I knew it had been an accident. Had I known he wasn't a dragon, I might have come up with an alternative solution, but I didn't know and sometimes we do unforgivable things in the heat of a situation. I had to forgive myself, though. Deep down I knew I was no murderer, and the whole thing had been a terrible accident. I ate my cake, which turned out to be as delicious as it looked, Sweetberry-chocolate flavour, with a light feeling in my heart. In an hour, this whole ordeal would be over, and I could go home a free woman. That was, if the jury took the same stance as the Ace.

When our hour was nearly up, we left the cafe through the main doors and not through the kitchen. It took us out into the main atrium again, and I was pleased to see the reporters still waiting by the kitchen door, checking their watches and tapping their feet. We managed to slip right by them without them noticing us and made our way back to Court Number One.

I was back in my place as the jury filed back in.

"Have you reached a verdict?" the Ace asked.

"Yes, Your Honour," one of the jury replied. He must have been designated the speaker.

"Was it unanimous?"

"No, Your Honour, seven voted one way and five, the other."

"Ok, the majority vote. Did you find Lady Club guilty or not guilty?"

I held my breath. It was a lot closer than I had anticipated, and I began to wonder if I hadn't celebrated too soon.

"Not guilty, Your Honour."

"Not guilty. Lady Club, you are free to leave." She hit her gavel on her desk.

I heard a cheer from the public gallery, which elicited an arched brow from the Ace, but I didn't care. I was free. I was officially not a murderer!

The journey home in the balloon was a much more joyful one than the one we'd made to get here. The air tasted sweeter and the land looked more beautiful even under its snowy blanket. I marvelled at the topography, and even the wintery storm clouds that were closing in with the promise of another dumping of snow were not enough to dampen my spirits.

We landed just outside of town as the storm was getting too close for comfort, and the balloon navigator didn't want to chance staying up in the air any longer than he had to. It was about an hour's walk to the castle through the snowy village, but as everything looked picture perfect and sparkling white, I didn't mind. Even when the clouds burst and we ended up in a blizzard, I couldn't shake the smile from my face. We were in eyesight of the castle when one of the staff came running up to us. I couldn't remember his name, but he was one of the youngest members of staff, barely a couple of years older than I. He looked out of breath as if he had run all the way from the castle, which he probably had.

"Willow, what is it?" my father asked.

"I saw the balloon land and was told to come get you as quickly as I could. The horses wouldn't budge in the snow, so I ran here. The troops are back your highness. There have been a lot of injuries, and I'm sorry to say, some fatalities."

"My sons?"

"Their highnesses are all home safe. Sage and Sequoia are uninjured, Ash has a broken leg and fractured elbow, but he is expected to make a full recovery."

My father's face took on a look of grim determination, and he picked up his pace towards the castle. I had to run to keep up. Willow followed alongside.

"Who was killed? Do you have names?" I asked, full of fear. I didn't want anyone to die, but the thought it might have been Oaken was unbearable.

"No Mi'lady. I only know that your brothers are safe. The injured are being treated in the main hall of the castle. The Queen has set up an emergency hospital in there, and healers have been brought in to help tend to the wounded.

Once back at the castle, I followed my father straight to the main hall. It had been filled with hundreds of beds, each one occupied. Healers were running from man to man, trying to help the most injured. I ran up and down the rows of beds, looking at each one to see if it held a boy with sandy coloured hair. I found my brother, Ash who was being bandaged up by a pretty young woman in a healer's uniform. As he was chatting away and joking with her, I assumed he was going to be all right. I spotted Star on the end of one of the rows and ran to her. A line of men waited to be seen by her.

"Hey," she said when she saw me. "You're back. How did it go?" She pressed down on the wrist of the man she was attending to, and he yelped with pain."

"Sorry," she said to him. "Possible fracture of the wrist. Go to the end of the hall on the right. They will sort you out." The man walked off and another replaced him. His head was covered in blood, and he had a few missing teeth.

"Triage," she said to me to explain what she was doing.

"I got acquitted. Have you seen Oaken? I can't see him in any of the beds."

"Who?" she asked before turning her attention to the bloodied man. "Are you feeling dizzy at all? Did you black out?"

"No and no. I've got a headache, though."

"Right, go to the left over there. I think the wound on your head is superficial. Head wounds always look worse than they are, and I think yours is just a scratch. The ladies over there will give you some water, and they'll clean you up. If you feel dizzy, come back to me."

"Oaken!" I said, then remembered that she'd probably never met him. "He's tall with sandy hair and blue eyes. Have you seen him?"

"I'm sorry, Rose, I don't think I have."

"If he's not here, where would he be?"

"If he's alive, he's been sent home. Everyone who wasn't badly injured was told to go home."

"Isn't there a register or something so we know who made it back?"

"I don't think so. One probably should have been made, but we were just too busy setting this up."

I cursed the lack of organisation and left the hall. I saw Tree and Slate walking towards me with an empty bed for the hall.

"Have either of you seen Oaken?" I asked, not expecting them to know.

"Who is Oaken?"

"Never mind." I didn't really want to ask, but I had to. "Where are the dead?"

"Those that died there were left on the battlefield," replied Tree " The Queen has ordered a recovery party to retrieve the bodies, but the snow is so thick now that it's probably going to be a few days before they get there. The few that died on the way back have been placed in the castle dungeon."

"Thanks!" I raced down the corridor and headed to the stairway to the dungeons. As much as I didn't want to find Oaken there, I had to know. As I reached the door that would lead down to the cellars, I heard my name being called behind me. I turned to find Sorrell racing down the corridor towards me.

"Thank goodness. I'd heard you'd got back. I saw Father, and he said that you'd been acquitted. That's fantastic!"

"Yeah!" I replied quickly and without interest. I felt anything but fantastic at the moment. I didn't want to talk to Sorrell; I wanted to go down into the cellar so I could find out if Oaken had survived.

"We could do with your help in the hall. I'm just heading there now. Oh, and I wouldn't go down to the cellar. That's where we have put the dead soldiers."

I couldn't tell her that's exactly why I wanted to go down to the cellar. She didn't give me the chance, though. She grabbed my arm and led me back to the main hall where she put me in charge of wound cleaning. With the long line of men waiting to be tended to, I'd be working late into the night. The euphoria of winning the trial had quickly dissipated to be replaced with worry. I asked every man I tended if they knew what had happened to Oaken, but none of them knew. Some were in too much pain to answer, and some were incoherent. I got the impression that the battle itself was just as disorganised as the castle was right then. No one really seemed to know exactly what had happened, but I was told that The Clubs had won. The Hearts had given a bloody fight but had eventually been beaten by the sheer numbers of Clubs. I was surprised to find that some of the men I tended to were injured Hearts who had been left to die by their own men. Ours had brought them home to be treated, not wanting them to die. It seemed strange to me that anyone would do this. Maybe the Club soldiers were just better people than I was. It was hours later, and I was beginning to flag. I looked up at the clock on the wall and realised it was almost five am. I'd been awake nearly twenty-four hours.

January 7th

"You need to go and get some rest, Rose," my mother said to me as I tried to stem the blood from one of the soldier's arms. She'd been saying the same thing to me for the past three hours, but I'd kept holding off, hoping that the next soldier would know if Oaken was alive. I was about to tell her that I'd stay up just a while longer when I realised I was practically nodding off. If I wasn't careful, I was going to cause more injury to one of these men due to extreme fatigue. I still hadn't been down to look at the bodies. Leaving now would give me the chance. I could quickly slip down there before I went to bed. Of course, If I did find his body, I'd not be able to sleep at all. It was a chance I was willing to take. I thanked my mother and slipped out of the hall. I was just about to turn left towards the dungeons when I heard my name being called. It was Willow, the boy who had run to find us in the snow.

"Hi, Willow."

"I was hoping to find you because someone handed me this to give to you." He handed me a brown paper parcel tied up with string.

"What is this?" A corner of it was damp as though the contents were wet or had leaked.

He shrugged his shoulders and turned, leaving me with the damp parcel.

Who on earth would be giving me something? I carefully ripped back the brown paper until I came to a note.

Dinner tomorrow night?

Underneath the note was a fish. Its scales gleamed in every colour of the rainbow.

I whooped for joy which was quickly followed by an angry looking healer poking their head through the hall doorway and telling me to be quiet.

I whispered an apology and, headed to the kitchen to give them the fish to prepare. If it was half as good as Oaken had said it was, I didn't want to waste it by trying to cook the thing myself. The head chef was surprised and almost excited when he saw what I'd handed to him and he promised to have it cooked to perfection in a meal for two.

I ran back upstairs towards my room but I was stopped by a loud knocking at the main castle door. Usually, a butler would open the door for us but the majority of the castle staff were in the hall tending to the sick.

I opened the door cautiously. There stood Oaken with the craziest looking bunch of twigs in his hand.

"I would have bought you flowers," he grinned, handing the twigs to me, "but the flowers are all under the snow. I had to improvise. Did you get my gift?"

I wanted to jump into his arms and kiss him after days of wondering if he was alright but I suddenly felt extremely shy in his presence. I'd dreamed about him for days but the truth was I barely knew him. My feet were glued to the ground and I found myself trembling. What a lousy warrior I'd make. I might have been able to fight off a dragon but nothing could have made me bridge the gap between Oaken and I.

I didn't need to. He stepped forward and placed his hand on my cheek. I could feel the roughness of it but it was warm despite the weather which had started to snow again. A snowflake landed on my eyelash and then another on the tip of my nose. Oaken moved forward and with the lightest of touches, kissed it away before pulling back.

"All gone!" he smiled, making those dimples appear but he didn't kiss me again. I waited, what felt like an eternity before I spoke.

"Will you kiss me again?"

"I don't need to. The snowflake has gone." He was teasing me. I'd never wished for a blizzard before but I was surely wishing for one now. Another snowflake landed on my cheek. He moved forward and, like before, kissed it away and moved back.

I couldn't wait for another snowflake to land on me, although they were coming thick and fast. One landed on his lower lip and, taking his lead, I moved forward to kiss it away. I started off softly as he had and I felt the snowflake melt, wetting our lips as it did. Unlike him, I didn't pull back and thankfully, this time, neither did he. I felt his tongue part my lips as the kiss became more insistant but then he pulled back again leaving me hungry for more.

"Will you kiss me again?" he asked as the snow swirled rapidly down around us.

"I don't need to." I replied, echoing his earlier words, and he looked at me quizzically.

"I'm never planning on stopping," and I moved forward, kissing him, knowing that whatever our futures held, all that mattered was now.

The End

The Three of Clubs

Stargazer Lily Club is the complete opposite of her sister. Where Rose is headstrong, Star is compliant, where Rose is brave, Star battles with fear, but, when she's the only one able to save her brother's life, she must conquer her fear and set out to get the medicine he needs. With The Queen of Hearts after her and the clock ticking, will Star get what she needs before time runs out

Available on Amazon now

Other books by J.A.Armitage

War and Suits Series (New Adult Urban Fantasy)

Three of Clubs

Four of Clubs

Five of Clubs

Six of Clubs

Guardians of The Light series (YA Paranormal Romance)

Endless Winter

Infinite Spring

Endless Summer

Autumn Ever After

Becoming Aethelu (prequel – only available to my newsletter subscribers)

The Labyrinthians Series (YA survival story)

The Labyrinthians

The Labyrinthian Diamond

The Labyrinthian Escape.

To find out about future releases, sign up to my newsletter at
www.J.A.Armitage.com

Made in the USA
Charleston, SC
27 September 2016